DEDICATION

I would like to dedicate this book to my mother Renee'.
Thank you for everything!

ACKNOWLEDGMENTS

As with everything I accomplish in life I would like to thank GOD first and foremost. He is the center of my life and from whom I gain all my strength and talent. His continued love and mercy towards me allow me to not only be the writer I am today but also the servant He asks me to be. Without Him I am nothing and I owe this all to Him.

To my husband, my hottie, my team Paige, the right side of my heart and the man GOD molded just for me I cannot thank you enough. You have been nothing but supportive, understanding, motivating, and generous with me on this journey. I can't think of an adjective to describe all that you are to me each and every day. Your love for me is unconditional and sharing my life with you is my greatest blessing. This journey is just one of many that we shall attack and conquer together and knowing that I have you on my side even when I'm being a meanymcmeany pants (insider) makes it all worthwhile!!! #teampaige #99moreyears

To my mother Renee' or should I say Susie B where to

start where to start??? I told you years ago that you are MY HERO and today that theory has been tried and proven true! The woman I am, the morals I possess, the drive I have, my focus, my faith, and my ability to love all stems from you! Imitation is the most sincere form of flattery and each day I attempt to emulate the woman you are is the true testament to your role in my life. I couldn't thank you for all you are, all you have been and all you will be if I had a thousand tongues!

To my daughter niece Taylor and daughter Tavia I couldn't begin to describe the impact you have on my life. My moves are calculated, my thoughts are considered carefully and my words chosen wisely to ensure I am the perfect role model to the both of you. Motherhood is a gift and journey that is not granted in the same form to everyone. You two have been my untraditional chance to experience such a blessing and I can only hope that at some point in life you realize just how much it means to me that you have taken me on this journey. As you continue to grow and become women in your own rights always remember that my love for you is unconditional, irreplaceable and never ending! I love you!!

To my brothers Norris and Renard or should I say 2nd and 3rd father (lol) your support and protection over the years allowed me to get this far in life with minimal bruises and broken hearts (mostly because you wouldn't let me date). Back then I didn't understand but now I have to admit that you're over protective ways have helped me in the decisions I make today. I love you both and thank you for all you've done for me.

To my aunt Antoinette THANK YOU for being my auntie, other mother and friend. Your support and encouragement through the years have been invaluable. I love you.

To my friends and family. THANK YOU for your love and support. I am not always easy to deal with, or get in touch with but I thank you all for your understanding and patience. I love each of you independently for different reasons but the love is still genuine and pure. I have encountered and interacted with each of you for different reasons, periods of time, and different circumstances and each of those interactions have created a memory that I could never forget. I love each of you!

To my coworkers thank you for continuing to believe in me and trust me enough to follow my lead. Your belief and support in me allows me to make decisions and trust my judgment because I know if I begin to sink or drown you will trust me enough to get us out of it. Your daily commitment to the team makes it all worthwhile and I owe my success to you! Thank you. Thank you. Thank you.

To Jessica Watkins thank you for this opportunity. The ability to share my talent with others was always a dream and now thanks to you that dream is now a reality and I am beyond grateful to you because of that.

To anyone I may have missed individually or as part of a group please forgive me and blame my head and not my heart. I know that my successes in life have not been independent achievements but exist abundantly as a result of group efforts thanks to so many people. I wish I could thank each of you separately but if I tried the acknowledgments would be longer than the book! (Lol☺) Please know that I love you all!!!

I hope you enjoy reading it as much as I enjoyed writing it!

Jessica Watkins Presents
Deceitful Vows

A. MACKIN

Prologue

Surprisingly Kayla did well for her first day back. Her patients actually found her more relatable and down to earth since she was no longer wearing a wedding band. She had only used FaceTime twice to check on how well MJ was doing with Virginia. Even when Mark called to see how she was holding up, she took the call like a champ. Although she missed her baby terribly, she had to admit she wasn't a nervous wreck like she'd thought she would be. The morning and early afternoon went smoothly until around two-thirty when things got ugly.

"Kayla, get home now! It's urgent! I'm on my way there!"

She couldn't get a word in edgewise before Mark hung up.

Click.

Kayla didn't know what to do or say. Her instincts kicked in, and she immediately grabbed her purse and flew out of the office. She paused for a brief moment to tell her assistant that she was gone for the day and would not be back. She pretended to ignore the sound of the young girl smacking her lips at her statement. Kayla didn't even know where she came from or who hired her and didn't much care at the time. Rebecca was her assistant before she went on maternity leave. Sometimes they switched personnel to make easier accommodations, so Kayla didn't think anything of it. But after working with Latoya for just half a day, she knew this arrangement wouldn't last long at all.

Kayla sped all the way home, doing at least eighty-five miles per hour on the highway. She made the usual forty-five minute drive in twenty minutes. She attempted to call Mark back several times but didn't get an answer. Once she pulled up to her home and saw cop cars everywhere, her heart started racing and everything instantly became blurred through the tears. Once she saw the ambulance come out with a gurney, she lost all focus of her car, and everything went black.

Seven months earlier...

Chapter 1

Driving up Interstate 95, Kayla realized that it was unusually sunny for January in Maryland. By no means was it anywhere near spring-like temperatures, but the brief relief from the snow was a well needed and welcomed change in weather. As she reached over to change radio stations, her ringing cell phone got her attention. Noticing the restricted number flashing on the Caller ID screen, Kayla hesitated. She inwardly debated with herself whether she should answer it or not. The ringing stopped briefly but only to begin again almost immediately. The unknown caller was persistent. So, reluctantly, Kayla pressed the power button.

"Hello?"

Only silence returned her greeting.

"Hello?"

Still silence.

"Hello?! *Hellooo?!*" Kayla screamed, thoroughly annoyed at the pushy caller who didn't have the decency to say anything.

After a sigh of frustration, she returned her attention to adjusting the radio. Her phone rang again. Assuming it was the relentless caller, she answered with frustration in her voice.

"Who is this?!"

"Whoa! Is that any way to greet your husband?"

Instantly, Kayla relaxed and smiled. Hearing Mark's voice was exactly what she needed after a rough morning and meeting with six of her less than classy patients. She needed a pick me up, and her man definitely did just that. Mark and Kayla had been married for just over a year, and they were very much still in their newlywed phase. The two had met at the gym during his daily workout routine to keep his body in tip-top shape. Kayla was on one of her "resolution" kicks. She was known to diet, workout, take a yoga class, or enroll in karate classes from time to time. Each activity was an attempt to take her mind off of her loneliness. She never stuck to any of those things or even went to more than three sessions. But whenever her friends or family back home asked what she was up to, Kayla took pride in rattling off her impressive list of activities.

"Kay? ... Kay?" Mark's voice pulled her out of her trance. "Are you listening?"

She hadn't heard a word he'd said. "I'm sorry, babe. I was watching the road. What did you say?"

"I'm going out for a drink with Wayne and Steve after the gym tonight, so I'll be home late."

"Oh...okay, sweetie. Have fun and text me so I know you're okay. I love you."

"I love you too," Mark said right before the line went dead.

Kayla was disappointed because she wanted to spend the evening with Mark, but she refused to be the wife that bitched every time her husband went out. So instead of taking him on a guilt trip, she sent a text to her bestie Stephanie.

Kayla: *Hey! Wanna go to ladies night? I need a drink!*

Within seconds, Stephanie responded: *Sorry...can't. I have a date! Wish me luck.* ☺

DECEITFUL VOWS

Kayla: *I want details! Emergency text?*

Stephanie: *I doubt it, but check in around nine o'clock just to make sure.*

It was official. Kayla was going to be alone tonight. So she decided to grab some pasta from a local Italian restaurant close to her house. She would eat it while watching a movie.

After pulling her 2014 black Range Rover up to her spacious and extravagant Churchville, Maryland, home, she exited the car, and offered a quick wave to her neighbor. She pitied the young woman who was struggling to carry two bags filled with groceries into her home.

The sun had gone down, bringing with it the reality that it was indeed winter. Kayla felt she was about to freeze to death, walking from the car to her front door. Once inside, she emptied her food onto a plate, popped a movie disc inside the DVD player, and settled on the sofa to relax and unwind from a long day. Mark would be home late, and she had a few hours to kill before she was expected to place the fake emergency call to Stephanie just in case she was having another horrible date. Kayla smiled, thinking about the last time she had to save Stephanie. She had gone out with an intern from her marketing company where she was a senior advertisement agent. The dude's tight butt and his handsome, clean-shaven face had impressed her so much that she overlooked a few small details. For starters, he had no car and he lived with his parents. Kayla had to come to Stephanie's rescue when his bank card was declined when he attempted to pay the bill for their date.

Kayla couldn't understand why her friend had such a hard time with men. She was a gorgeous sistah with dark mocha skin and the biggest almond shaped eyes. Her lips were full, and she had a nose so perfect that it looked cosmetically designed. Stephanie's naturally curly hair was compliments of her African American and Hispanic genes. Her hair stylist maintained its warm brown tint, which went perfectly with her skin tone. Standing barely four inches above five feet at about one hundred and forty-five pounds, she was considered thick in all the right places. And her booty could stop traffic. Yet Stephanie hadn't had a serious relationship in the three years. Kayla could tell it was really starting to take a toll on her. Last year at her wedding, she wasn't sure if Stephanie's tears were tears of joy or jealous sorrow. After all, Mark and Kayla had met, dated, and gotten married within two years. During that period of time, Chris, Stephanie's ex, decided to leave her for his neighbor. Trying to help her heartbroken girlfriend get over her ex and forget about men altogether, Kayla decided to take Stephanie out for drinks one evening. Ironically, it was the night that Kayla met Mark. She reluctantly took his number while Stephanie was in the bathroom so she wouldn't seem like a totally insensitive friend. After a few pleasant phone conversations, she agreed to go out with him the following weekend. A year later he proposed and the year after that, they were married. Now a year into their marriage, Kayla still wrestled with the guilt of meeting her prince in the midst of her best friend's heartbreak. Over the years, Kayla had attempted to fix Stephanie up with several guys. She even introduced her to a few of Mark's friends, but there were no love connections. Why Stephanie was still single was a huge mystery that Kayla was destined to solve. Her happiness as Mrs. Mark Barnes was the most wonderful feeling she'd ever experienced in her life. And she wanted to bask in her joy and share it with her best friend.

Kayla's cell phone chime brought her out of trip down memory lane. She looked down and saw a text message from Mark. Instantly, she smiled at how sweet it was for her man to actually keep his word by letting her know that he was okay. The smile on Kayla's face was quickly replaced with a deadly scowl and butterflies in her stomach as she read the screen.

Mark: *Sorry running late. I'll be there soon. Can't wait to see you.* His signature smiley face followed.

Where was he running late to and who couldn't he wait to see? All kinds of thoughts began to race through Kayla's mind. What the hell was Mark doing? Where was he? Who is he with? Suddenly, it felt like the wind had been knocked out of her. She had to lean on the kitchen counter to keep from falling when her knees buckled. Kayla took long deep breaths to try to regain control of her body. Her cell phone chimed again. This time it was Stephanie.

Stephanie: *Having fun. No emergency call needed. I'll call tomorrow.*

Knowing that Steph was okay momentarily took her mind off of Mark. But it was only short lived. Within seconds, she found herself in the middle of the dining room floor sobbing uncontrollably. An hour later she picked herself up off the floor and went upstairs to shower, hoping that her tears would blend with the shower spray and wash away the deceit she was sure her husband was up to right down the drain.

Chapter 2

Friday morning Kayla woke up feeling like a bus had hit her. All of the crying from the night before had left her with a massive headache and huge bags under her eyes. She crawled out of bed and went to the bathroom to release her bladder and see just how much damage her blubbering had done to her face. She could smell the coffee pot brewing, and she heard the cabinets opening and closing downstairs in the kitchen. After relieving herself, washing her face and brushing her teeth, she went downstairs in search of the awesome aroma of hazelnut. She had almost forgotten about last night until she saw Mark.

Kayla stopped dead in her tracks and took in the sight of her six-foot-two, two hundred and twenty-five pound husband. His light cocoa skin was smooth and shiny. As if he could feel her staring, he turned around all of a sudden and flashed her a smile, displaying all thirty-two pearly whites. Although Mark was five years older than Kayla, at thirty-two years old, his consistent workout regimen kept him buff and toned. He wore his hair cut low and faded and always dressed in expensive suits. He wouldn't be caught dead without his signature cologne, 1 Million. To Kayla, Mark resembled the actor Michael Early because of his sexy eyes. And whenever his hair grew out a few inches, it curled on the ends.

Kayla met her husband's gaze and gave him a smile that didn't quite reach her eyes. Realizing that last night was not a dream, she decided to inquire about his evening. "How was your night? I didn't even hear you come in. It must've been pretty late when you finally got here."

"Oh yeah, babe...my fault. It was a little late. Those niggas ain't want to shut up, and I didn't want to bother you, so I stayed downstairs." Then, Mark stuffed a piece of toast in his mouth and avoided Kayla's eyes.

Kayla knew something was up. Mark *never* talked urban smack. He often used slang to annoy her and make her drop conversations because he knew how much it bothered her. Determined to uncover whatever her husband was hiding and get to the bottom of it, she pushed the issue. "So you only went to *Friday's* to have wings and a few beers with your boys? Well...oookay, " Kayla said slowly before she turned and headed for the steps so that she could get ready for work.

As she climbed the stairs, a nagging feeling churned in the pit of her stomach. Although she couldn't put her finger on it, Kayla knew there was something her husband wasn't telling her and she had to find out what it was.

****

She walked into her office confidently with her usual bright-eyed smile and cheery attitude. Although her marriage may have been on the rocks, she had only one rule when it came down to her attitude in the office: Never let them see you sweat. Kayla was the youngest and the only African-American psychologist in her office. She landed the position right out of graduate school. While her co-workers considered their patients as pathetic welfare recipients who only wanted to defraud the state out of eight hundred dollars a month, Kayla looked at them as young women in need of guidance or simply someone to talk to. She maintained the biggest caseload in the agency, but it wasn't because she was naïve enough to believe that her peers respected her. Kayla took pride in helping the young women she counseled. On Fridays, she didn't see patients, though. She spent the day reviewing notes and cases in preparation for the following week. She also made calls to some of her more at-risk patients who needed a little more TLC, just to check in with them. This morning Kayla walked in with no intention of making any special calls. She had no plans to review a bunch of notes either. There was something more pressing on her mind...like saving her marriage.

Kayla made it a habit not to call Mark when he was showing a piece of property. It was his job, and she believed he should be left alone when conducting business. Mark was a top commercial real estate investor in his family's firm. He had followed in his father's footsteps and was next in line to take Mr. Jack Barnes' position as CEO of Barnes Real Estate in a couple of months. After the out of place text last night and Mark's strange behavior this morning, Kayla was anxious to find out what was going on. She called his phone, and it rang three times before it rolled over to the voicemail. Finding that strange, she decided to send him a text message instead.

Kayla: *Hey! I was thinking date night tonight with my sexy husband.*
Mark: *Maybe...I might have to show a property later.*
She inserted a sad face before the words: *Okay. I miss you.*
Mark: *C'mon Kay don't do that. This is a big deal I'm working on.*
Kayla: *I know. I still miss you.*
Mark: *As soon as I close this deal we can go on a vacation. Just pick*

a place.

Kayla: *OK. Enjoy your day. Until tonight...*

Slumping down in her office chair, all kinds of thoughts ran through Kayla's mind. On one hand, she was aware of how hard Mark worked to make things easy for them. On the other hand, she still couldn't get that text message out of her head. She tried hard to reflect on Mark's behavior over the last few weeks. There had been no signs of an affair. But then again, she never pried or tried to chain him to a leash. So he always had plenty of room to mess around, and she wouldn't have been the wiser. Realizing that she was going to be on her own tonight, she decided to go out. There was a romantic comedy in theaters that she'd been dying to see for weeks. But since Mark wasn't into those types of movies, he had refused to take her. Kayla purchased a ticket online and headed out the door. She hated standing in long lines at the movies, especially on a busy Friday night. The Kiosk was out of the question. It seemed she always got stuck behind someone who had no idea what they were doing. Once the system came up, Kayla logged onto her online banking first. Financially, she and Mark were good on cash. Considering how much she had struggled all through college, she now enjoyed looking at the zeroes in her bank account to remind her of how far she'd come. Once the Bank of America screen loaded up, and Kayla saw her accounts, she smiled to herself. She was about to log off, satisfied with her balances, but her credit card balance caught her eye. Actually, it was Mark's card, but because she was an authorized user on it, she was able to view the balance also. Taking note of $387.13 balance, she decided to schedule the payment. Neither she nor Mark liked to carry balances on their credit cards. Because he often forgot to schedule the payments, he'd added Kayla to the account for that purpose. She was good at keeping up with the finances and making sure everything got paid on time.

Kayla clicked the hyperlink to go into the account and instantly turned red. The building started spinning, and she felt like she was about to vomit. Staring back at her was a hotel charge for the Marriot Hotel and a purchase at Fogo De Chao, the popular Brazilian steakhouse. Both charges had been made on the same day. Immediately, Kayla began thumbing through her text messages to try to figure out where Mark was *supposed* to have been on that particular day. She ruled out that these purchases were work right away. Kayla was certain of that because Mark hadn't used his corporate credit card for either transaction as he usually did for business. He never stayed in a hotel as long as his business took place in the state of Maryland. He always made his way home no matter what. The hotel stay and the meal at Fogo De Chao had been personal. She was sure of it. It was painful for Kayla to receive, but Mark had been entertaining someone—more than likely, another woman.

Finally, she reached the series of text messages that she and Mark had exchanged on that particular day. According to the text messages, he was supposed to have been in Richmond, Virginia, working on a deal to buy the space for a big new outlet mall. Without warning, a whirlwind of emotions overtook Kayla. She went into an uncontrollable bout of tears and sobs. It didn't matter that she was at work, breaking her number one rule. Her professionalism had flown out the window. Kayla's heart shattered into a million pieces, and her reputation no longer mattered. In fact, *nothing* mattered anymore. The love of her life...her soul mate...the man who had vowed to love her unconditionally until death, had broken his vow to her. And she was completely clueless as to what to do about it.

After discovering the text messages that Mark had sent her in an attempt to cover up his cheating ways, Kayla drove home in a blur. She vaguely remembered getting permission to leave the office early for the day. At the time, she was an emotional train wreck. All she wanted was to arrive home, crawl into her comfortable bed and sleep her life away.

***

The smell of bacon, eggs, and coffee filled Kayla's nostrils the next morning, alerting her that her cheating husband was home. She tried to get up, but she wasn't really ready to face Mark just yet. A few minutes later, he entered the bedroom with a tray of food in his hands and a smile on his face. Kayla wondered how someone so deceitful could do it with such a straight face. Mark sat the tray down and went to draw the blinds open to let a little sunlight in the room. Kayla had to admit that her husband looked very handsome in a pair of True Religion jeans hanging low on his waist and a black Ralph Lauren polo shirt. His overall appearance was quite casual for a day at the office. Before putting a piece of bacon in her mouth, Kayla took the opportunity to inquire about last night, considering she had slept most of the day away. "So how did the meeting go?"

"It went well. We should close in the next sixty days."

"That's good. I'm sure Jack will be excited to finish one last big deal before he retires. And I'll be excited that I get my husband back."

"Yeah, my dad is pretty happy about it."

"So what time did you get in exactly? I don't remember hearing you come in."

"It was pretty early actually. I was in by eight-thirty."

"I must've been beat. I don't remember a thing. So, what do you want to do today? I was thinking we could go look at some new patio furniture."

"Babe, you don't remember? I have to help my dad start clearing out some things from the office this morning. It shouldn't be long, though. But when I'm done, we can go do whatever you want to do."

"Oh yeah..." Kayla lied slow and deliberately. She hadn't remembered that at all. In fact, she recalled Melissa telling her that she and Jack were going skiing this weekend in the Poconos. Mark's mother wasn't exactly in love with the fact that he had chosen Kayla for his wife. Melissa had hoped he would choose a girl from their side of the tracks with a better pedigree. It didn't matter that Kayla had earned two degrees and wasn't what one might consider ghetto. She simply wasn't from the suburbs, and her family didn't fit into their social circle. Neither parent earned a six-figure salary, nor were they privy to certain luxuries in life. They couldn't afford a service staff or exotic vacations. Vivian and William Todd were plain old middle class. She was a sixth grade history teacher, and William was a foreman for a local construction company in Pittsburgh where Kayla grew up. Mr. and Mrs. Todd had worked hard to give Kayla and her sister, Courtney, very comfortable lives. The Todd sisters never wanted for anything. And they were showered with lots of love and attention. Because Vivian was an educator, academics were very important in the Todd household.

However, Kayla's education and successful career weren't good enough for Melissa. She simply believed that Mark could've found a woman from a better family with connections to high society. Therefore, Kayla had not been fully accepted into her family or her social circle. Melissa and Kayla only spoke to one another out of cordialness—nothing more and nothing less. Any and all of their conversations were purely for the sake of keeping their men happy. Kayla's guess was that this was her husband's *"lie of the day."* Mark knew that there was no way Kayla would want to go with him or call to confirm his story since it would mean possibly seeing or speaking to Melissa. What Mark didn't know was that last week she had run into Melissa leaving out of the bank. During their brief chat, his mother had mentioned that she and his father were going skiing this coming weekend. She had insisted that they join them for dinner the following weekend after they return home. Mark was also clueless that Kayla had woken up the night before during the time he allegedly should have been home and discovered he was not. Normally, Kayla wouldn't have given any of this a second thought, but after the text messages and the charges to the credit card, she knew something was up. And she was determined to figure out exactly what it was.

Chapter 3

After eating only half of the breakfast Mark had prepared and served her, Kayla showered and got dressed. Keeping it simple, she put on a casual white blouse with jeans and wedge heel knee boots. She swept her hair up into a messy bun and was ready to head out the door. Known for wearing very little makeup, she applied a coat of lip gloss in the car. Kayla was a natural beauty, without exotic features like slanted eyes or high cheek bones. She had caramel colored skin, which was free of all traces of acne and blemishes. She had big brown eyes, full lips, and her nose did make her look like she had some form of island decent but to her knowledge she did not. Kayla was petite in stature, standing a few inches above five feet. She only 5'3" and weighed around one hundred and twenty-seven pounds. She was far from having a video girl body shape, but her full 36DD's gave her small frame just enough enhancement to make her stand out. Kayla didn't mind that she didn't have any super special features about her to make her stand out over the top. She enjoyed that she could still turn heads without having to spend hours in the mirror to make it happen. Kayla often kept her shoulder length hair pulled up or back. Very seldom did she wear it down.

After pulling out of the driveway, Kayla found herself driving to the only person she could share her recent concerns about her husband with.

Thirty minutes later Kayla pulled up to Stephanie's condo and got out. The cool brisk winter air hit her, and she welcomed the breeze instead of running from it. Lately, she had been feeling like she was suffocating, and finally she was able to breathe.

It felt good.

After greeting the doorman and taking the elevator up to the thirteenth floor, the familiar suffocating feeling suddenly came back. She had difficulty breathing again, and she had the urge to vomit. Kayla ran from the elevator to Stephanie's door. She knocked continuously and consecutively until her friend appeared. Sprinting past her, she reached the half-bathroom down the hallway in time to empty her entire breakfast in the commode.

"Do you need water?" Stephanie asked from the threshold.

"I do. Thank you."

"What brings you here so early and what happened to you?"

"I didn't know where else to go or who else to talk to," Kayla answered, wiping her mouth with tissue.

Immediately, Kayla broke down and poured her heart out to Stephanie.

"Why would he do this to me? We make love at least five times a week, we go out on dates, and I don't nag him about working all the time. I'm the same woman he married. I just don't understand why he would do this to me."

"C'mon don't do this to yourself. You aren't even sure if he's having an affair. You're just assuming he is. Don't drive yourself crazy over a thought."

"It's a strong thought. He was supposed to be in Richmond that weekend, not at the Marriott or at some restaurant eating. The fact that he put it on his credit card knowing that I could see the statement shows me that he doesn't care anymore. He didn't even try to hide it. What if he wants to leave me for her? What would I do without him? He is my whole world, and I would die if he left me!"

"Kayla Barnes, let me tell you something right now! You will *not* blame yourself for the actions of a trifling ass man. I told you he was no good. He thinks with his little head, not his big head, like most men. What you have to realize sweetie is that men love new pussy and there's nothing you can say or do to change that."

Kayla noticed Stephanie staring off as she talked to her. Kayla knew that this whole ordeal was taking Stephanie back to when her ex cheated on her. She felt bad for sending her friend on a trip back down memory lane but appreciated the support she was getting.

It felt good for her to be able to tell someone else about the pain she was experiencing. Kayla continued to talk for what seemed like hours and now that the words were coming out of her mouth, she was convinced that her husband was having an affair, and she knew she had to confront him and get the truth.

Stephanie listened to her best friend of the last four years cry her heart out about her husband. The day of the wedding, Stephanie tried to warn her about him, but Kayla had insisted that she was in love and Stephanie was wrong in her thoughts about Mark. Kayla blamed Stephanie's doubt about her future husband on the pain from her recent breakup with Chris. Stephanie and Chris dated for two years. Stephanie was ready to settle down but Chris was just warming up to the idea. He cheated on her with several women. The breakup with Chris caused her to hate all men. Stephanie was certain that Mark was a liar and a cheater.

She knew it wasn't a good time to say, "I told you so," because that would only break Kayla's heart more. So instead, she just listened and rubbed her best friend's hair while she poured her heart out, all the while thinking that not only was her friend right about her thoughts of her husband but she would sure enough end up heartbroken.

***

Less than an hour later, Kayla found herself walking around the Inner Harbor aimlessly. Stephanie had listened to her story and offered her support, but she couldn't spend very much time with her. Chad, her new beau, was going to take her to the National Harbor to spend the day, and she was running late because of Kayla's breakdown session.

Kayla did a little shopping and got a bite to eat at the Cheesecake Factory before heading back home. Once again left alone with her thoughts and tears, she decided to give her husband a call. After just two rings, he answered, and despite the fact he was an adulterer, she smiled when she heard his voice.

"Hello?"

"Hey, babe. What you doin'?"

"Nothing much. I just got to the office. I'm about to start packing some of the old man's things."

Kayla cringed. "After thirty years, I'm sure there's a lot to pack."

"Trust me. It is, but we have time. He won't officially retire for a few more months, so we don't have to do it all today. What're you up to?"

"I just left Steph's condo. Now I'm at home watching a movie."

"Oh really? You just left Steph's condo?" Mark replied in a mocking tone.

"Don't do that, babe. You know that's my girl."

"Yeah, I know. It still doesn't mean that I have to like her. But I know she's your girl."

"Why can't the two of you get along?"

"Look, babe, I have to go. I don't want to be here all day. I'll see you later."

"Okay, babe. I'll see you later."

It was crazy to Kayla how, even though, there were so many signs of infidelity there, she still couldn't stop smiling like a school girl whenever she spoke to Mark. She stopped scrolling through the TV Guide channel and finally settled on a Lifetime movie. She had slept half of yesterday away, and she had only been up a few hours today, but it didn't take long for sleep to overcome her.

Kayla was awakened to Mark tracing his warm tongue around her sweet spot. He was licking and tracing imaginary words around her inner thighs while rolling her nipples in between his thumb and index finger. Soft moans escaped her lips as he continued to lick her slowly. He moved from her thighs to her opening and began to suck and lick her clit. The feeling of what he was doing in between her legs and what he was doing to her breast caused her breathing to become shallow and her heart rate to increase. She tugged and rubbed at his head, encouraging him to go deeper as she felt her orgasm begin to build. Without warning, her soft moans turned into slight screams and she felt her body trembling. In a split second, she felt her hot orgasm oozing out, and nothing else could be heard in the room except Mark slurping up her juices. Satisfied with the orgasm she'd just had, Mark flipped Kayla over and plunged deep inside her with just one thrust. Kayla's walls quickly tightened around him, fitting him like a glove. With each stroke, she arched her back more and tried to keep up with him, not wanting to cum again so quickly. She reached back, grabbing his shirt, causing him to stop stroking. Once he stopped, she began rocking her back to him, getting her rhythm and bouncing her ass up and down on him just like he liked it. She released his shirt and allowed him to stroke her. It wasn't long before he realized that at this pace his orgasm would quickly approach. So Mark pulled out, flipped her back around and threw her legs over his shoulder once again, and entered her. Kayla arched her back, letting him go deeper, and he knew he couldn't hold out any longer. Her juices were now spilling out, and she was digging deeper and deeper into his back. Before he knew it, Mark was grunting and bucking like a wild horse, releasing his seed deep inside Kayla before collapsing on top of her.

After their impromptu lovemaking, Kayla decided not to spoil the mood with questions and accusations about him having an affair. Instead she laid underneath her husband, basking in the afterglow and silently praying that she was wrong about his cheating ways.

***

Continuous chimes woke Kayla out of her sleep. Looking around in the dark room, she realized that it was Mark's phone. Sliding from underneath his comatose like body, she quickly picked up the phone and silenced it. Not seeing the name on the Caller ID screen, her interest piqued. So she attempted to unlock it. After trying his birthday, her birthday, their anniversary, and address, she decided to try his safety net—his parents' address. After typing in the four-digit house number to his childhood home, she was able to see ten new text messages. Kayla took the phone into the master bathroom to read the messages in secret. She figured she needed to sit down to read them. She sat on the commode and pushed the message icon.

I had a great time today, the first message said.
I'm sorry you couldn't stay longer.
I wish you would tell her and get it over with.
Brunch tomorrow?
You could make up for leaving me early today.
You home yet?
You must be.
Talk to you tomorrow.
I love you.
Good night

Unable to contain herself any longer, Kayla stormed out of the bathroom and pounced onto Mark like a wild animal who had just stalked their prey. Surprised and caught off guard, he tried to get up and defend himself, but surprisingly, his strength was no match for Kayla's anger.

"Who the fuck is she?!" Kayla screamed loud enough to wake up anyone in a two-mile vicinity.

"What? Who is who?" Mark asked looking confused and scared at the same time. "What are you talking about?"

"*Her*! Who the fuck is she?!" Kayla responded now with a pool of tears streaming down her face. "And why is she sending these messages?!"

"I don't know what you're talking about, Kay! Just get off me so we can talk."

"I'm not moving until you tell me who she is!" Kayla spat as they wrestled with one another.

"She's nobody!"

"She has to be somebody! She's telling you that she loves you, that she should tell me about the two of you, and that she had a good time today! A nobody would not have that much to say! Who is she?!"

Mark didn't say anything. He just kept fighting to get up.

Seeing that Mark didn't appear to have an answer for the question, Kayla continued. "Is she the same person you were with at the Marriot and Fogo De Chao?"

Instantly, he froze. Panic and fear came across Mark's face, and Kayla knew that she was right. She had her answer. In a more calm tone, she asked the question that would decide the fate of her marriage. "Do you love her?"

Instead of answering her question, he simply looked away. That was it. That was all she needed to know.

Their marriage was over. There was no way to stay married to a man who loved someone else. So slowly Kayla got up and started up the stairs. Mark sat confused and in silence. Not once did he go after her, nor did he try to explain anything. He just sat there. Even when she came down with luggage the first time, he didn't move. The second time she brought more bags, he still didn't move. When she came to retrieve her cell phone from the coffee table in front him, he didn't bother to make eye contact. Mark didn't move from the sofa until he heard her car engine start and was sure she had pulled away. Finally, he went to the window to confirm what he already knew. His wife had left him.

Chapter 4

Kayla only made it to the bottom of the street before her emotions got the best of her again. Barely able to breathe, she didn't know what to do. Going back home was not an option. There was no way she could look in the face of the man who had lied to her and deceived her for the last three years. Sitting in her car in the middle of the night crying was also something she could not do. She quickly grabbed a napkin from the glove compartment and wiped her eyes and face. Then she began driving again. A few minutes later, she found herself pulling off of Interstate 95 and into a Days Inn parking lot. Slowly she climbed out of the car and grabbed the smallest suitcase from her trunk. After checking in and paying with cash, she retreated to the room with the king size bed and full bathtub she had just rented for the night. Kayla had every intention of relaxing in a nice hot bath and then getting a good night's sleep while she planned her next move in life. With so many emotions and nerves running through her body, neither of those things happened. She was too restless to bathe, and sleep did not come easy.

***

Mark awoke to the sound of his alarm going off. He rolled over and checked his cell phone.

Nothing.

There were no missed calls or text messages from Kayla. He wasn't sure why he didn't answer her question last night. After all, he did not love the other woman. In fact, it had started out as just the opposite. But somewhere down the line, after a few nights of sex and dinner dates, things changed. While he was certain he was not in love with her, he would have been telling a lie if he said he felt nothing for her at all. Presently, he was caught up in his own web of deceit, and he had no idea just how much Kayla knew about it. On one hand, he had his wife, whom he truly loved. Kayla was Mark's heart. He just couldn't understand why she didn't accept that his career came first. He worked very hard so that she didn't have to. He wanted his wife to enjoy life without having to work all day. Yes, he wanted three or four kids. Their children would attend private school and would require a nanny, chef, and a piano teacher. One couldn't afford such luxuries without hard work. That's exactly what he was doing. Kayla refused to quit her job, although her income did not matter very much in their household. Kayla could blow her entire paycheck on a single handbag, and it wouldn't make a difference to Mark at all. He allowed Kayla to work in order for her to feel that she was contributing to their style of living. He hated when she brought her work home with her. Mark was tired of hearing about her hood rat clients, who were pretending to suffer from postpartum depression, or some form of bipolar disorder just to collect a welfare check. Although he grew up in an affluent community where he didn't experience that life firsthand, he had heard of stories about women who gave birth to babies just so they could live off of the system. Some women depended on others for shelter, food, medical coverage, and money for their survival. Those types of women sickened Mark. He loathed the idea that his wife helped those kind of women for a living. In his profession, he offered revenue for the government, and jobs to people like Kayla's clients. So at the end of the day, Mark wanted to come home to a hot meal and good sex. He didn't want takeout from different restaurants and stories about Shaquita and her fifth fatherless child. Unfortunately, as of late, that's all he'd been getting.

"She," on the other hand, was different. She had a job that made sense. Her income allowed her to live a comfortable lifestyle. It was also one of her biggest pitfalls. With the other woman, Mark didn't have to listen to stories of underprivileged women while eating takeout meals. Instead, he had the luxury of hearing stories of million dollar ads being put together over homemade dinners. The best part was usually before he could finish his meal, she had his dick in her mouth. He loved the wild, kinky, spontaneous sex he shared with his secret lover. There was no nagging, no hair rollers, or cuddling before and after sex. It was just sex. Mark knew it couldn't go on forever, though. Eventually, the other woman would want more, and he wasn't sure she was worth it. Recently, he had started taking her out on dates. Before cutting ties with her completely, he needed to make sure that she wasn't someone who he could be with long term. Lord knows she would be easier to take home to his mother. To Mark's surprise, she wasn't bad outside of the bedroom. She was also nothing like Kayla. No matter where they went or what they did, she didn't hold a candle to his wife. Kayla was humble and down to earth and even though he didn't approve of the type of women she helped, he admired her kind heart and warm spirit. Mark wondered why he had allowed Kayla to leave last night when she was the one he truly loved.

Maybe his affair with his mistress meant more to him than he thought.

***

It was almost noon the next day when Kayla finally woke up from her slumber. The growling of her stomach reminded her that she hadn't eaten since yesterday at the Cheesecake Factory. Her lack of food also caused her to feel queasy and dizzy. She almost fell when she stood from the bed. Realizing that she had to eat soon, Kayla quickly showered and threw on some sweats and sneakers. She pulled her hair back into a ponytail, grabbed her bags, and headed out of the room. After checking out of the hotel, she went to Panera Bread café and ate a bowl of soup and a half of sandwich. Although she was famished from the day before she wasn't quite ready for a heavy meal. While wallowing in self-pity over her meal, she made up her mind about her next destination. She decided not to call her parents. She wanted her visit to be a surprise to them.

Kayla checked her cell phone, hoping that Mark had called or sent her a text message. He hadn't tried to reach her at all. His lack of interest helped Kayla come to a much-needed conclusion. Her mind was officially made up. Kayla called her boss and requested a week off to deal with some personal issues. Because she rarely took time off from her job, Mr. Nicholson approved her request. He told her she could take as much time as she needed and offered her his support. After speaking with her boss, Kayla left the café to start her journey to Pittsburgh.

A few hours and a couple bathroom breaks later, Kayla finally arrived at her parents' home. It felt good to be in a familiar environment. The deceit in her home and Mark's betrayal had left her emotionally drained. Kayla grabbed her bags from the trunk of the car and walked to the front door of her childhood home. Her mother had made very few changes to the house since she was a child. Kayla's room was pretty much still the way she had left it. Because she lived closer to Pittsburgh than Courtney did, Kayla visited her parents often. Courtney had moved to Atlanta right after nursing school, and she only came home on the holidays if her work schedule allowed her to. Her bedroom was now Vivian's home office where she prepared her students' lessons and graded their papers. It was also where she'd go to get away from William from time to time. They had been married twenty-nine years, and even though they were still madly in love, Vivian needed a break every once in a while.

Kayla rang the doorbell and waited patiently for someone to answer.

Vivian came to the door wearing her favorite apron with a spoon in her hand. "Kayla, baby, what are you doing here?! Come on in!" She turned and yelled over her shoulder, "William, guess who's here? It's Kayla!"

Kayla hadn't visited her parents since Thanksgiving. She and Mark started alternating holidays between their families when they first started dating. Since Kayla's parents were out of state, there was no way they could see both families on the same day, so they spent Thanksgiving in Pittsburgh and Christmas in Maryland.

Finally, looking up from the Steelers versus Browns game on TV, William got up and gave his daughter a hug. He truly admired the woman his baby girl had grown up to be. He always took pride in bragging about her to his work crews.

William knew that something was wrong the minute he laid eyes on Kayla. He had made it a point to keep smiles on Kayla and Courtney's faces. It had been his desire to show his girls how a man was supposed to love and treat a woman. He sent Vivian flowers all the time and took her out on dates regularly. He also helped her with the housework and cooked meals for her often. Vivian never complained about being bored or alone. William did those things out of love for his wife, who he truly adored, and to show his girls what their future husbands should do for them. Kayla didn't have to tell William about Melissa's ill feelings toward her. He'd noticed her bad attitude the first time they met. He wasn't one to pry, so he didn't push or make a fuss about it. But he never forgot it either. Now, as Kayla stood before him looking heartbroken, he wondered if Melissa was the reason for his baby girl's visit.

Kayla stood nervously shifting her weight from one foot to the other. She knew her dad was aware that something was wrong. She could fool her mom, but not her dad. Kayla was closer to her dad than her mom. Growing up he spoiled her rotten, often giving her things after her mom had refused to. Therefore, naturally, she confided in him more. She could never lie to William because he always knew the truth. She stood in place and waited for him to get up. She fidgeted and hoped he didn't ask too many questions in front of her mom. She wasn't prepared to tell either of her parents why she was really there, but definitely not her mom. If she had to talk at all, she'd prefer to speak with her dad.

"Baby girl!" he said excitedly after turning around and reaching out to her.

"Daddy!" Kayla said, almost matching his tone and stepping into his embrace.

This was the most comfort Kayla felt in a long time. William sensed it too and let her rest on his chest a little longer.

"What brings you here, sweetheart?" he finally asked, sitting back down in his recliner.

"Nothing much...just missed you guys. I'm off work for a few days, so I decided to come spend some time with you guys."

"But it's Sunday, baby girl. You know we have to work tomorrow. Why didn't you come Friday?"

"Oh, William hush," Vivian chimed in. "It doesn't matter what day she came. I'm just glad she's here." She smiled from ear to ear. She was obviously happy Kayla had come to visit them. "Come help me in the kitchen, baby. I'm making pork chops, macaroni and cheese, and collard greens for dinner."

"Sure, Mom. Just let me wash my hands, and I'll be right there."

Vivian headed to the kitchen to finish dinner, and Kayla carried her bags upstairs. After plopping down on her old bed, she checked her cell phone again. Still nothing. She wasn't sure if she should've been angry or worried at this point. She decided to be neither. Instead, she washed her hands and went to help her mom in the kitchen.

"So...are you excited or worried?" Vivian asked as soon as Kayla sat down and started grating the block of the cheese she'd found on the cutting board.

"Am I excited or worried about what?" Kayla asked confused. She hoped that Vivian didn't notice that something was wrong.

"The baby..." Vivian whispered.

"What baby?" Kayla asked with a confused look on her face.

"Oh, child, please! You may be close to your daddy, but I'm a *woman* and a woman always knows. Sweetheart, you're pregnant!"

Chapter 5

Lying across the bed sad, confused, and heartbroken, Kayla had no idea what to do. She had gone to CVS Pharmacy after dinner to get some toiletries that she'd left behind in haste to leave home. She also picked up a home pregnancy test after having that talk with her mom. Initially, she had dismissed the idea of being pregnant altogether. Then she explored the possibility. At first she contributed her constant sleeping to stress. She blamed her sudden dizziness and queasiness on her poor eating habits. The vomiting, she believed, was a reaction to Mark's unfaithfulness. But nothing could explain the positive result she got from all *three* pregnancy tests she'd taken in her parents' bathroom. Kayla didn't know what to do. She was pregnant with an adulterer's baby. Her husband had not only met someone else, but he'd lied to her about the woman. He had been keeping secrets. And he had obviously fallen in love with another woman. His wife is now at her parents' house heartbroken and pregnant with his child.

"Could things get any worse?" Kayla asked aloud after letting out a long, exasperating sigh.

***

It had been three days since Kayla left Mark. She still had not heard a word from him. She was up packing her things, preparing to leave Pittsburgh that evening. Her parents had been respectful by not asking her any questions about Mark during her visit. They assumed when she wanted to talk about it she would. In the meantime, they went along with her little game.

Kayla knew she had to leave that day. There was no way she could explain why she was still there when her parents got home from work. She would have to tell them the truth, and she had no intention of doing that...at least not yet. She hadn't confirmed her pregnancy to her mom. She still hadn't accepted it herself. Of course, she wanted kids. She and Mark had even discussed it, but the plan was to wait until he took over his family's company. Then she would cut back on her work hours so that she could raise their kids. Kayla didn't believe in nannies, so no matter what, Mark had agreed that she would be allowed to raise the kids and work. It hadn't been easy convincing Mark to agree to her terms because he was a firm believer in nannies and housekeepers. He had been raised that way. He'd only accepted Kayla's idea in order to get the children he wanted. He wanted three little ones running around the house. He was sure that eventually, Kayla would change her mind and welcome some help. After packing the last items in her suitcase, she loaded it in her trunk. She went back inside to make a sandwich before her drive back home. Now that she knew that she was eating for two, she was much more conscious of her eating habits.

Mark was going crazy. It had been three days since Kayla had left. He was lost. At first, he thought she was just blowing off steam. He also thought she was trying to teach him a lesson. But now he was convinced that Kayla was really gone. It wasn't supposed to have gone this far.

Mark sat in the living room on the sofa in complete silence. He was truly lost. He hadn't eaten, slept, showered or worked in three days. All he'd done was watch his phone, hoping she'd call. She hadn't. Mark wanted Kayla back, but he just didn't know how to get her. His pride was so strong that he couldn't even imagine begging her to come back. His ego was so big that he couldn't bring himself to make the first call. The walls were closing in on him. He couldn't live without her, so he had to do something soon.

His cell phone chime pulled him from his daze. Holding his breath, he looked at the display. It was *her*, the other woman. He let out an annoyed sigh and sent it to voicemail. She had been calling for days, but he'd refused to answer. After all, this was *her* fault. Kayla was gone because he'd gotten caught up in her web. He didn't want to talk to her at all. He wanted his wife back.

***

During the drive back to Baltimore, Kayla drove in silence. She had to decide on her future plans. If not for her, she had to for her baby. She needed to know what role Mark would play. Abortion was not an option, and neither was adoption. Kayla was going to have her baby with or without Mark.

Halfway through the drive, it dawned on her that she had nowhere to go. She wasn't ready to go back to her house, and she wasn't in love with the idea of staying in another hotel.

She picked up her cell to call Stephanie. She hadn't spoken to her since the day she'd told her about Mark's affair. Typically, that meant that Steph was really into whoever she was dating at the time. Kayla figured that she could crash at her best friend's crib for the night and catch up with her. After all, she needed some good news in her life.

Stephanie answered on the second ring, sounding a little down herself. "Hello?"

"Hey, sweetie. How's it going?"

"Good. How are you? Did you fix things with Mark?"

"The opposite. Now I saw the *proof* in black and white."

"Proof?" Stephanie sounded alert and focused.

"Yeah *proof*," Kayla said, laughing a little. It amazed her how gossip always perked her friend right up.

"Can I crash at your place tonight? I've been gone for three days now, and I'm not ready to go home just yet."

"Of course you can. Come on over. I'll leave the door open for you."

Kayla hung up with Stephanie, feeling relieved already. At least she had somewhere to stay and someone to talk to tonight.

After pulling up to Stephanie's condo, she finally got upstairs with her luggage. Unsure when she would be leaving, she brought all three bags with her. She'd planned on just one night, but she knew that could possibly change.

"I thought you asked if you could you stay the night," Stephanie said as she stood in the doorway watching her friend bring in her bags. "It looks like you're moving in!"

"I know, but I don't know when or if I'm going back home."

Stephanie waved Kayla off dismissively. "Yes, you do. You love the dirt on the bottom of that Negro's shoes, so you're going back."

"You're right. I do love him, and I do want to go back, but I also love my baby. I have to think about him, or her, first."

Stephanie's mouth flew wide open, and shock was written all over her face. She mustered up the energy to say congratulations, but Kayla couldn't tell if it was genuine or not. For a second, she felt a twinge of jealousy coming from Stephanie, which was odd. She and Stephanie had had many conversations over the years about having kids. Although Kayla wanted kids as much as Mark, she wasn't in a rush to become barefoot and pregnant.

She quickly dismissed Stephanie's reaction, assuming it was out of concern over the recent problems in her marriage.

The two friends spent the next three hours catching up. Kayla told her about the text messages and Mark's reaction when she asked if he loved the other woman. She also told her about the visit to her parents' house and how she found out about the pregnancy. Stephanie filled her in on Chad and what they were up to. Kayla was a little surprised because they hadn't been together as much as she'd thought they would be, but she hadn't really heard from Stephanie. Stephanie explained that his work schedule was pretty demanding. Although she really liked him, she wasn't sure if that was something she was ready to compromise with him on. Stephanie was used to guys banging her door down and blowing up her phone. So if Chad wasn't doing either, Kayla was sure that Stephanie was contemplating giving him the boot. After they were up to speed on each other, they ordered Chinese takeout and watched old movies.

Around three o'clock in the morning, Kayla got up to use the bathroom. Lately, it seemed like all she wanted to do was sleep or pee. So far, the pregnancy wasn't really affecting her. When she thought about it, she'd been having the same symptoms all along. But now that she knew why, her symptoms were at an all-time high. Besides those few times she'd vomited before she found out that she was pregnant, Kayla hadn't been sick. Tomorrow would be her first visit with her OB/GYN. Dr. Gallant's receptionist had been able to fit her in quickly since she was already a patient. Kayla was nervous and excited. She was curious to see the life growing inside of her, the life that had been created on top of lies and deception. She assumed she was around eight to ten weeks based on her last cycle and the information from the internet. According to Google, she would be able to hear the baby's heartbeat tomorrow. Kayla wished that Mark could be there to hear the first sounds of their baby too, but he still hadn't called or sent any text messages. Kayla refused to reach out to him first because he was the guilty one who couldn't keep his dick inside his pants. After washing her hands and returning to Stephanie's guest bedroom, Kayla made up her mind that tomorrow after she saw Dr. Gallant, she would search for a new home. Her marriage had already been destroyed, but every day she stayed gone solidified the fact that she would be a single parent. Being with a liar, an adulterer, and a deceitful man was not a part of Kayla's dream, but she vowed that her child would know who his or her father was. Even though she couldn't stand the thought of Mark, she knew that allowing him to share her pregnancy was the right thing to do. It wasn't for her and not even for him. It was all about the baby. Kayla was determined to be a good mother, even if it meant she had to deal with Mark. Her child's happiness and well-being was all that mattered now. So tomorrow after the appointment, she would call Mark and share the good news...*their* good news.

She just prayed to God that he was willing to accept it.

Chapter 6

The buzzing of the alarm told Mark that it was morning and it was time to get up. He'd decided last night, after finally showering and eating, that he would call Kayla today. He missed her terribly and he was ready to put his pride aside to save his marriage. He only hoped that Kayla wanted the same.

But first he showered and got ready for his meeting. The buyers for the new outlet mall had asked their accountants to review the budget that Mark had presented them a few weeks ago, and they were finally ready to negotiate. Mark was hoping that they would agree to the terms, so that they could close the deal soon. The entire project had been in the works for months. It was the main reason why Kayla had felt neglected. If everything went well today in the meeting, Mark could tell her the good news tonight to help improve his chances of convincing her to come back home.

Originally, he'd planned to make a reservation at a new Italian restaurant that had opened close to their house, but he quickly decided against it. Kayla didn't like to discuss personal issues in public. He even proposed to her at home when it was just the two of them, so that they could discuss things before she agreed. Smiling to himself at the memory of the proposal, he hurried to grab his briefcase and keys to head out the door. He definitely didn't want to be late to the meeting. It was important that he seal the pending deal. It wasn't just for the company's profit, but it would solidify his role as the next CEO and save his marriage. After setting the alarm and checking for his cell phone, Mark headed out the door to meet with the man who could change his life.

***

Morning came too quickly for Kayla. She'd had another restless night and she really wanted to just lay around and watch television. But she had an appointment with Dr. Gallant. Later, she would tell Mark about the baby.

She got up and made her way out of bed. After dressing in jeans, an oversized sweater, and a pair of booties, Kayla grabbed her purse and cell phone and headed out the door. She sent Steph a text message to let her know that she'd locked up the condo and that she would call later before she came back over. It felt odd to her that Step left without saying a word to her that morning, especially knowing that she had her first prenatal appointment. Kayla made a mental note to ask her about it later. She knew that Steph had her issues with Chad on her mind. But she was sure it was more to things than her friend had told her. Having her own issues to deal with, Kayla decided that she needed to at least find a temporary furnished apartment today, so that she could give Steph back her privacy. Two women with man problems under the same roof was a recipe for disaster.

Pulling up to Dr. Gallant's office, Kayla parked and went inside. Today's weather was not on her side. Therefore, a casual stroll was out of the question.

She had to think of a way to tell Mark about the baby. Originally, she planned to ask him to meet her downtown at the Harbor since her doctor's office was close by. However, the temperature wasn't cooperating. She needed to find another place to tell him.

After signing in with the receptionist and paying her copayment, Kayla took a seat and began to think of where she could meet Mark to talk. She wanted to do it in a public place in case his reaction wasn't a happy one. However, she didn't like to discuss personal things in public settings. She decided on the Starbucks a few blocks away from the doctor's office. It was midday, so most people would've already had their morning fix, which meant there wouldn't be a lot of traffic, hustling, and bustling. It would be quiet enough so that she could talk without yelling. Deciding that Starbucks would be the perfect place, she sent Mark a text message right before the nurse called her name to go in the back to see the doctor.

***

Mark's smile spread from one ear to the other after reading the text message from Kayla. She wanted to meet and discuss something with him in about an hour at the Starbucks close by. Mark had just finalized the big deal for the mall. Mark couldn't contain his excitement after reading the text message. He tuned out everything happening in the room around him. The only thing he was concerned about was what he planned to say to Kayla once he saw her. He knew he would have to leave the meeting early, but he was certain that the remaining business on the table would go well. Thirty minutes later, he excused himself from the group of businessmen, explaining that he had an emergency he needed to tend to. Understanding his position within the company, the buyers excused him. His accountant assured him that he would be able to seal the deal. Leaving the meeting early would allow Mark time to get to the coffee shop and clear his head before Kayla arrived. He knew that the meeting could make or break his marriage.

***

Dr. Gallant moved the ultrasound machine around the cold gel on Kayla's stomach confirming what she had assumed. She was indeed nine weeks pregnant and her little one had a strong solid heartbeat. Kayla allowed the tears of joy to escape. She had always wanted kids, but never thought she would feel the excitement and love she felt after she saw that tiny heartbeat. She now had to make decisions for the life growing inside of her. She was determined to protect her baby at all costs. After getting a prescription for prenatal vitamins and making her next appointment, Kayla left the doctor's office to make her way to Starbucks for her meeting with Mark. Dr. Gallant had printed two photos of the baby and gave them to her as keepsakes. Surprisingly, Kayla was excited to show them to Mark.

Arriving at Starbucks, Kayla found Mark already sitting at a table with two drinks sitting on the table in front of him. She made her way to him with a smile on her face. When she got closer, she smelled his Polo Blue cologne. He stood to greet her with an embrace. Kayla wasn't sure if it was the hormones or the fact that she hadn't seen him in days.

Regardless, she fell into his arms and stayed much longer than she'd planned. Realizing that they were nestled up long enough, she stepped back and admired him in his navy blue suit with the cufflinks she had given him as a birthday present the year before. His crisp white shirt with navy, light blue, and grey stripes complemented him well. She was reminded that today was the big day with the investors. Kayla knew her husband well. Whenever he wore a blue or grey suit, it meant money was on the line so he was dressing the part. Kayla took a seat at the table and moved the nonfat vanilla latte with an extra shot to the side. Noticing that she didn't acknowledge the drink, Mark started pleading his case just like he had been rehearsing before he lost his nerve.

He opened his mouth to start his speech, but Kayla blurted out, "I'm pregnant!" before he had a chance to say a word.

Chapter 7

"Wow! *Really*? I'm going to be a daddy!" Mark yelled out with a look of joy and excitement on his face that Kayla had never witnessed before...not even on their wedding day.

"Shhhhh! Lower your voice, Mark. We are in *public*," Kayla said through gritted teeth while looking around to make sure Mark hadn't formed an audience. It was precisely why she didn't like talking about personal things in public. She didn't want a crowd of people there to buy coffee sharing in her pregnancy news. If Mark could've been the loyal faithful husband he'd promised he would be, they would be celebrating the news in the comfort of their home over a home cooked meal like normal people. Instead, they were at a coffee shop like strangers meeting for their first date.

"Yes, Mark, you're going to be a daddy. I just left Dr. Gallants office. We're nine weeks pregnant, and the baby is due around Labor Day!" Kayla said with excitement.

Seeing the look on her face and the excitement in her voice, Mark knew he had to make things right for his family. His wife was having a baby, and he needed to be there for them instead of somewhere else with someone else. Kayla pulled out the sonogram photos and showed Mark the baby's early images. She also let him know when the next appointment was and invited him so that he could experience the miracle growing inside of her. The two sat for the next hour discussing plans for their baby and Kayla's workload. She was planning to go back to work on Monday. She would tell her boss about the pregnancy.

However, she wasn't making any plans to slow down just yet. She was feeling great so far and she didn't want to cut back too early when it wasn't necessary. Mark let her know that the mall deal went through so without having to work all those additional hours he would be free a lot more to be there for her and the baby.

***

While the two sat and talked about what the next few months of their life would be like, they had no idea that *she* was watching and planning her next move. It was supposed to be *her* baby and not Kayla's. She had been poking holes in the condoms, trying to get pregnant. Kayla hadn't been trying to conceive at all. She knew how bad Mark wanted kids, and wondered what kind of wife she was to not honor his request. Now, by chance or accident, Kayla was about to give Mark the one thing he wanted more than anything else. Now that Kayla was pregnant, there was no way that Mark would leave her now. The mistress needed to put a plan in place quickly before she lost her man for good.

***

Mark and Kayla left Starbucks to get lunch at another location. The two were talking about life and the baby the entire time. Kayla knew she would have to address the elephant in the room, but she would wait until after she had eaten. Mark offered her something to eat at Starbucks after he realized why she wasn't drinking her latte. But once she said she needed a meal because she was famished he didn't hesitate to suggest that they go to lunch. They went to a popular deli where they both ordered sandwiches and a fruit cup for Kayla.

"Tell me why Mark," Kayla said, out of what seemed like nowhere.

Of course they both knew what she meant, but since their arrival she had only talked about her plans for the nursery. Wanting to make sure that he didn't say anything to make matters worse, Mark took a deep breath and began explaining himself.

Reaching across the table, Mark placed his hands on top of hers. Initially, she was hesitant to touch his, but she finally relaxed and allowed him to caress her hand as he spoke. "Kayla, I'm really sorry for what I did to you, baby. You have to believe me," Mark said through teary eyes before he continued. "You are always paying more attention to your clients than us. You leave home before me and you get in after me, and yet you still bring your work home. We don't have sex as much as we used to and when we do its never spontaneous or exciting. Kayla, I love you with everything in me, but it's like we've been married for twenty years or something. It's getting boring and dull."

By now Kayla pulled her hand away and stared Mark directly in his eyes. Lowering his head to finish his speech because he couldn't stand to see the look of hurt on her face he continued to talk. "I just don't understand why you insist on working to help those hood rat females. Why won't you just stay home and be a mother?"

That was all she could take in listening to Mark tell her why he had the affair. Within seconds, she found her lunch coming back up. She had to make a mad dash to the bathroom to keep it from landing all over the café floor.

While wiping her face and rinsing her mouth out with the tap water, Kayla couldn't hold back the tears that wanted to escape. Right there in Au Bon Pain, she cried her soul out. Her wails were so loud that a worker of the café knocked on the door to make sure she was okay. Seeing the commotion at the bathroom door, Mark shamefully dropped his head. All the while, he'd spoken as if he were justified in his ways, expressing that if Kayla had been a better wife then he would not have needed "her." Now his pregnant wife was in a public bathroom crying hysterically over an affair he seemingly had no remorse for or regards for her feelings. Kayla's reactions to the information made Mark look like the scum of the earth. Twenty minutes later, Kayla finally came out of the bathroom to face Mark. She could see the look of guilt and remorse in his face. It was much more evident than the night she left. She wasn't sure if the new found regret was because of the affair itself or because of the baby, but either way she was glad that it was there. Her knowledge that he had hurt her and not cared was a bigger pill to swallow than knowing the hurt happened in the first place. Kayla found some truth to some of the things Mark said about their marriage. Some things were evident. Some she didn't realize until he brought it to her attention. But she knew that his affair was out of line and he was completely wrong for it. She would be lying to herself if she didn't admit that they did have a few problems. Trusting him again would be a work in progress, but for the sake of her family, she realized that she had to at least give it a chance. She sat back down at the table with her husband, who was the reason her marriage was in shambles.

"Mark, I love you, and I believed in our marriage whole heartedly. I never intended for you to feel any of those things you felt, and I never intentionally placed anyone ahead of us. None of what you said justifies you sleeping with someone else and jeopardizing our marriage. If running away, lying, cheating and deceiving me is what you believe, the resolution is to, by all means, end things right here and right now. However, if you are saying that it was an isolated incident and you want to truly spend the rest of your life with your child and me, then we can try to make this work. Please know that I do not trust you. This is not the only discussion we will have about this and we will seek counseling, but I am willing to try if that is what you want."

***

Mark let out the breath he was holding in for the last two minutes that Kayla was talking. He didn't realize it until he felt himself exhale that he was even holding his breath. He had no idea what she would say when she returned and he'd been spending the entire time preparing yet another speech to explain things to her. Hearing her agree to try was exactly what he needed to hear. If his wife wanted to make things work by any means, that's what he was going to do. His life from this moment on was going to revolve around Kayla and their children.

Chapter 8

After Mark and Kayla stayed at Au Bon Pain a little longer, talking about the conditions of the reconciliation, they parted from each other. Kayla wanted to stop by her office to check messages and emails. Although she wasn't going back to work until Monday, she still didn't want anything to wait. She could review some notes at home and plan to meet with her patients first thing Monday morning. She also wanted to let her boss, Mr. Nicholson, know about the pregnancy and the time she would need off for her next appointment.

After checking her messages and emails, Kayla packed a few files in her bag to take with her. Surprisingly, she didn't have much to review. Her patients seemed to be okay with rescheduling during the two weeks that she was out and didn't leave any urgencies with Kayla's assistant for her to follow up on.

Maybe they are all faking, Kayla thought for a brief second, and then quickly dismissed the thought. Maybe her patients didn't have textbook psychological issues, but they definitely needed someone to help them and she was that someone.

Kayla locked her office back up and knocked on Mr. Nicholson's door on her way out. He was a middle-aged white man who had been managing the office for over twenty years. He always wore nice suits and kept his salt and pepper hair tapered low. Kayla couldn't understand why he'd stayed at this office for so long when the majority of the clients were African American, and would always throw race and discrimination into their claim whenever he denied them benefits. He'd had a fair share of threats thrown his way and once someone even keyed his car and flattened his tires. That never stopped him from coming in though. He simply put his car in the repair shop, got a rental car and was back at work the next day. Once, when she had her first denial and the woman accused him of not signing off on it because she was black, Kayla asked him was he racist.

Her boss' response was simply, "I help people, not colors. Caucasian folks ask for assistance as well. Just because it's not as many in this area doesn't mean they don't exist. I make recommendations based on the individual, not the color. I'm not racist at all. I'm here to help, simple as that. I won't allow someone to run me away from doing what I love."

Kayla didn't understand it before, but she did after his explanation. All types of people had come in asking for help, and she had to admit that Mr. Nicholson was always fair in his decisions. He had denied several Caucasian people as well, without batting an eye. Kayla admired his work ethic and enjoyed working under him.

After telling him about the pregnancy and her next doctor's appointment, Kayla headed out to go home and begin piecing her marriage back together.

***

Since Kayla decided to work on her marriage, she was going back home. So, she needed to stop by and get her things from Stephanie's house. She sent a text message to let Stephanie know that she was on her way.

Kayla*: Hey! Wanted to stop by and pick up my things. Is the alarm code the same? I can use my spare key.*
Stephanie*: It is, but I'm already home so just come on over.*

Kayla wondered why Stephanie was home so early but figured that she'd taken another half day at work. In Stephanie's company, her presence in the office wasn't essential. She could pretty much work from anywhere she wanted as long as she pulled in the contracts. Kayla wondered why Stephanie didn't open her own firm since she was the reason the company had as many big accounts as it did. Stephanie once told her that if she opened her own company that would make her the boss and she would actually have to show up to work. She liked this arrangement better. Laughing to herself while thinking about her friend, Kayla pulled up to go in and repack her bags to go back home. She couldn't help but hope that this would be the last packing she would be doing for a while.

Stephanie greeted Kayla at the door when she got upstairs. To her surprise, all her things were packed and waiting. Kayla didn't intend to pack and leave so quickly. She wanted to at least sit and talk for a while, but Stephanie looked like she had other plans. She was dressed in a bodycon dress with stiletto knee boots and a full face of makeup. Kayla knew that Stephanie was headed out, but she decided to bring up her doctor's appointment, even though Stephanie looked like she really wanted to leave.

"Steph, what's up?" Kayla asked with her eyebrow raised as she watched Stephanie bring all of her bags closer to the door. "You didn't ask about my first appointment, and you left this morning without saying goodbye."

***

"What?" Stephanie was obviously agitated and annoyed that Kayla would even bring the issue up. She was so tired of everything about their friendship revolving around Kayla. Everything had always been about her. First it was her job, then her dating Mark, then her marrying Mark, then her being a newlywed, and now this baby. Stephanie couldn't remember the last time her friend talked to her about anything except herself.

Stephanie had known all along that Kayla got Mark's number the night they'd all met. She could tell as soon as she came back from the bathroom. It had hurt Stephanie when Kayla lied and said that she'd met him outside of her office. As soon as she'd introduced them, Stephanie instantly knew he was the fine brother from the bar that kept sending drinks to them that night. It was at that moment that she knew her friend only cared about herself, and she was sick and tired of it.

That brief trip down memory lane added more rage to Stephanie's attitude, and it was evident when she opened her mouth to talk. "I left because I have to work. Unlike you, I don't have a no good husband to support me, so I have to work to pay for this condo you're standing in and that Mercedes parked outside. Sorry that I didn't stop to check on your five minute pregnancy, but I had things to do. Just like right now. So if you don't mind getting your things so that I can get to work, it would be much appreciated."

Kayla had no idea where any of Stephanie's attitude or anger was coming from. She knew that she would be upset that she was going back to Mark, but she never expected her to speak to her that way. She couldn't figure out what had gotten into Stephanie lately, but she knew she didn't like it and had to figure out what was going on.

She had just decided to fix her marriage and now here she was fighting with her best friend.

She just couldn't win for losing lately.

***

Mark was at home anxiously waiting for Kayla to pull up. She was only supposed to stop by her office then head home. She had been gone for hours, and he was hoping that she didn't change her mind about the reconciliation, so he sent her a text message to make sure:

Can't wait until you get home. I miss you already... ☺

Since he was waiting on Kayla to return, he decided to start dinner to keep him occupied. He put on a pot of water to boil the noodles and pulled some ground turkey out to brown for the spaghetti sauce. He figured spaghetti and garlic bread was easy enough to not mess up and still would show Kayla that he was trying. They were out of wine but that was okay since Kayla couldn't drink anyway, so that wouldn't kill the mood. He poured himself some Hennessey and mixed it with Coke. He made it a double, drinking enough for the both of them.

His cell phone chimed, alerting him to a text message and he quickly grabbed his phone hoping Kayla responded that she missed him too. Instead, it was a photo from "her." She was naked and oiled down just like he used to like it. He was done with her, but he couldn't stop admiring her body. These types of pictures were a big part of how she lured him from the beginning. Kayla would never send something like that to him, and he would be lying if he said that he didn't enjoy the photos. He enjoyed it so much that his manhood stood at attention immediately.

***

Kayla walked in the door with her suitcase to find that Mark had started dinner and was deep into reviewing emails. The water was boiling, and the turkey was browning, but Mark was so consumed in the message from his accountant that he was neglecting the pots on the stove.

"Mark! Mark!" Kayla yelled rushing to turn the boiling water down and to turn the saucepan off.

Mark finally snapped out his thoughts and, realizing what was happening, he rushed over to the stove. Grabbing a potholder and reaching around Kayla, he quickly grabbed the saucepan to move it to another burner. Brushing up against Kayla, she felt his erection and couldn't help but blush.

"Looks like someone missed me," she said with a devilish smile. Watching her husband cook with a rock hard penis instantly made her panties moist. Even with all the drama of their marriage, she was still

54

undeniably attracted to him and couldn't resist the temptation. Thinking back to what he'd said about the spontaneity and passion in their marriage, she decided to act on impulse and satisfy her man.

As soon as he turned back around from the stove, she quickly switched off the burners and pulled down the Ralph Lauren pajamas he was wearing. It was an added bonus that he had nothing else underneath. The sight of his ten-inch erection and the scent of his Axe shower gel was all that was present as she took all of him in her mouth right there in the kitchen.

Mark's hands seemed to have a mind of their own from the way that he roamed all over her head or the loud moans escaping his mouth. The difference was that Kayla was deep throating him like never before. The slurping sounds she made intensified along with his shaft growing longer and longer in her mouth. The fullness of him was nowhere to be seen. He quickly lost control and shot his load down her throat. She swallowed it all, not missing a beat and pulled back long enough to lick her lips and wink at him.

Kayla was proud of herself. Never before would she have sucked her husband's penis in broad daylight in the kitchen. Nor would she have attempted to put as much of it in her mouth as she did. And she wouldn't have dreamed of swallowing his entire load. Something about their recent problems made her want to do more to satisfy her man. His reward for the effort was that he now had her bent over the kitchen island dipping in and out of her treasure pot with ease. She had no idea that pleasing him orally that way would make her so wet. Now she was getting her back blown out and Mark was having a hard time controlling his orgasm because she was so wet.

"Right there, Mark. Don't move. I'm cumming, baby. I'm about to cum!" were the last words Kayla said before Mark drilled her one last time before shooting his load inside of her.

If she wasn't pregnant before, she definitely would be after that one.

After their session, Kayla suggested heading upstairs for round two. Mark stayed behind to make sure the stove was off, and the door was locked. He also needed a minute to delete that photo from his phone. He silently thanked God for the door chime from the alarm system that alerted him to toggle from the erotic photo to his emails before Kayla walked up and saw it. As if it wasn't bad enough that the picture aroused him in the first place, he just made love to his wife with the image of that photo in his mind. That's when he knew this was going to be harder than he thought as he headed upstairs to make love to his wife again.

Chapter 9

Things between Mark and Kayla had been on the up and up since her first night home. The two were like newlyweds all over again. They couldn't keep their hands off of each other and Kayla was always suggesting something new and exciting to try. Mark loved the new effort his wife was putting into pleasing him. He couldn't help but wonder if he'd gotten this same treatment months ago if he had just simply asked for it, instead of stepping out on her in the first place.

Kayla wrapped up another day at the office with her patients. Now seven and half months pregnant and extremely agitated, she didn't have the same patience for her patients that she'd had before. She wasn't sure if it was the hormones or the reality of her job getting to her.

She was hurrying home to Mark because tonight they were going out to dinner to celebrate the official retirement of his father. Mark was now the CEO of Barnes Real Estate. Although the company was family owned, Mark worked very hard to get there and now that he'd made it, he'd vowed to take the company and his marriage to the next level. Kayla was sure that being a CEO was hard work, but staying true to his word, he had been more available to Kayla also. He hadn't missed a doctor's appointment yet, and he was home almost every night for dinner. It had still been takeout meals, but he never complained. Having his wife and unborn son at home was all he needed. So what from time to time he would look at the photo of "her" to help get off when he was alone. As long as he wasn't touching, no harm was being done.

***

She pulled into the parking lot, glad to see that his car was still there in its usual spot. Of course she had to drive around to park a little further back from the front spaces reserved for the CEO, CFO and the few other vice presidents, but she didn't mind the walk to the office. She strolled in and headed straight to the elevator being a familiar face at the company. Heading up to the 8th floor, she pulled out her compact and checked her makeup and her teeth for the spinach that she'd had for lunch. Satisfied with her looks, she put away the mirror and smoothed out her sundress. For some reason, she was nervous. She hadn't seen him in months, and she wasn't sure if he'd like the surprise. With the July heat, she'd decided on a very thin dress that she didn't require a bra. And for the purpose of the visit, her panties were nonexistent as well.

She got off the elevator and was glad she'd decided to wear her flat Michael Kors studded sandals so that her footsteps weren't loud against the floor. She was relieved to see that the receptionist was not at her desk in front of the office.

Good. One less nosy person to speak to, she thought as she headed to the office.

Turning the door knob, she was surprised that it was unlocked, but even more surprised by the sight she saw once the door was open.

***

Quickly pushing Monica away from him and pulling his pants up, he could have kicked himself for not locking the door. Mark was once again getting one of his daily treats from his new assistant, Monica. He stayed true to his word about not seeing "her" again, but that didn't stop him from getting blowjobs from the woman who scheduled his meetings. At first, Mark would ignore her advances when she would come in wearing short skirts and bare legs. He found it interesting one day, when she came in to review his calendar, that she did not cross her legs when she sat, but gave him a good view of her freshly waxed pearl. That was the day it all started. Not being able to focus on what she was saying from staring so hard, he gave up and told her that they would review the calendar the next day. Obvious that Monica was seducing him, she wasted no time in her attempt to straddle him. Mark was able to ignore that advance, but when she'd tried again, he couldn't resist. He gave into temptation, and a rock hard penis greeted her. She wasted no time in sucking and slurping him away. After that day, Mark was getting a blowjob two or three times a week. This was the first time he'd ever gotten caught.

***

Monica felt bad about what had just happened. Never did she think someone would just barge in the office. Of course, this had happened hundreds of time before, but today was the first time anyone had seen.

Mark never had to worry about Monica telling their secret. She didn't do it because she wanted to be with him or ruin his marriage. She gave him blowjobs because he showed his gratitude in her paychecks. There was no way she could afford her daughter's private school tuition on her salary alone. So if sucking Mark down meant a better paycheck and a few "bonuses" here and there, that's what she was willing to do. By no means was she saying he wasn't attractive or appealing. He was. But she had seen men like him before. Men like Mark could have the entire world at his feet, and he would still need or want more. Monica knew he would never leave his wife. In fact, she never asked or expected it. As long as she got what she needed from their little arrangement, she was satisfied and would continue to play her role, even if that meant smiling in Kayla's face when she came to the office. Now she had a feeling she would need a plan B because once "she" saw her and Mark together, she knew it was only a matter of time before the truth came out.

***

Kayla got home in just enough time to shower and change for dinner. In the beginning, she was doing well with the pregnancy but now, in the third trimester, it was really starting to take a toll on her. She had to go shopping for a whole new wardrobe because even things from her second trimester didn't fit anymore. Her face was getting fat, and her feet were constantly swelling. She only had three pair of shoes that she could fit, and none of them had a heel. It was also getting hard for her to keep up with her new found sex drive with Mark, but she refused to give up. He loved the new her, and the truth was she did too, but lately she hadn't felt as attractive and that basketball size belly she was carrying around was making it virtually impossible. Knowing that her marriage was still in a delicate place, she sucked it up and began applying her makeup for tonight's event. Whether she felt like it or not, she was going to be there for her husband in whatever way he wanted her to.

***

After finishing up at the office, Mark headed home to get ready for the evening. He kept thinking back to earlier in the day when he got caught with Monica's face in his crotch. He was glad to know that Monica wasn't out to destroy his marriage. She assured him that whatever story he wanted to tell about what happened she would confirm it. They knew it was both of their words against "hers." And since she would have to explain why she was there in the first place, Mark knew she wouldn't be too quick to open her mouth. He made a mental note to be more discreet about things and definitely make it a habit of locking the door to his office. Ironically, after being caught, cutting the affair off altogether never crossed his mind.

Mark found Kayla sitting at the vanity applying her makeup. He stood for a moment, and took in the sight of his now glowing wife. He could tell that the pregnancy was taking its toll on her. She wasn't complaining, but he could tell that she was uncomfortable. Truth be told, so was he. They still had sex, but he didn't feel that it was natural because her growing belly was always in the way. Though he appreciated her efforts, he wasn't as turned on as he had been in the beginning. And because of his lack of attraction for her, he still would go back to the photo in order to be with her.

Noticing him standing there, Kayla spoke up. "Are you just going to stand there and watch me, or are you going to come say hello?"

Mark couldn't help but smile, wondering how she knew he was there with her back turned to him.

As if she was reading his mind, she said, "I smell your cologne."

Her senses were severely heightened. With the pregnancy and, even though, the scent was nine hours old, he knew that it was still as fresh to her as when he'd gotten out of the shower.

Walking over to greet his wife, Mark felt guilty for the first time in months about seeing Monica. Watching Kayla trying so hard to satisfy him while carrying his son, should've made him want to do right all along. Instead, it allowed him to selfishly add another conquest to his list of infidelities.

Mark leaned down to hug her and kissed the top of her head. Extending her arms as best she could to return his embrace her heightened senses kicked in again. This time instead of smelling just his Polo Blue cologne, she smelled the feminine scent of Light Blue by Dolce and Gabbana. Immediately, her suspicions and hormones went into overdrive, and the rage was coming on strong. She took slow deep breaths to calm her nerves. Mark mistook her breaths as pain.

"Are you okay?" he asked.

While she wanted to respond, all she could say was, "It hurts," as she cried a pool full of tears.

Not knowing what was wrong, Mark asked, "Do you want me to call the doctor?"

In between sobs, she managed to say, "No. I just need to lie down."

He helped her over to the bed and out of her dress so that she could lay down. Initially, she declined water, tea, and food and opted to just lay there in her own tears as thoughts of her husband being back up to his old tricks weighed heavily on her mind. Eventually, she took the offer for water in order to get a moment to herself.

Mark headed downstairs to get the water that she'd asked for. One minute, they were talking and Kayla was doing her makeup. The next, she was crying hysterically saying it hurts but not saying what hurts or why. Kayla knew that Mark's frantic pace confirmed that he had no idea of what had just happened.

By the time Mark returned with the glass of water, Kayla had cried herself to sleep.

Chapter 10

Waking up to a painful headache, Kayla was reminded of the last night's events. Her already fragile marriage seemed to be on the rocks once again. Kayla knew she wasn't going crazy. She smelled the perfume, clear as day, on Mark's chest. Because the fragrance was so common she had no problem pin-pointing exactly which scent it was. The questions in her head was should she question Mark about it or wait to get more evidence? As she wobbled to the shower, she thought about what she would do. Once she was out in the hallway heading to the bathroom, she could tell Mark was still home from the smell of coffee being brewed downstairs. That was a surprise. Usually he'd be gone to the office by then. Instead of inquiring about his late start, she headed to the bathroom to get showered and to plan her next move.

***

Her: *Is that why I haven't heard from you? You're with the cheap slut now!*

Her: *You need to meet me at the Marriott at 1, or I'm sending the photos to your wife.*

Her: *You know I'm serious, so don't try to play games with me.*

Mark couldn't help but to shake his head and let out an exasperating sigh after reading the messages. Not only was "she" still trying to be with him, but now she was blackmailing him. Of course, he had to go meet her. He couldn't let his precious Kayla see those photos. Of course, she knew about the affair, and it was old news, but if Kayla found out who she was he would never get his wife back, and his marriage would officially be over. He didn't know how, but he had to find a way to make her leave him and Kayla alone for good.

***

She felt confident after sending the messages. Of course he would come; he didn't want his precious Kayla to find out who she was. The shock would be if he found out the photos weren't of them two together, but instead of him with Monica. Her true intentions for meeting him today were to seduce him. They were supposed to talk about the past and how they once felt about each other. She would bring up old places and things they did before he would have her for lunch on his desk. Meanwhile, she would have her phone recording everything from the minute she got off the elevator. She would then have the recording for the future in case she needed it to get him to leave Kayla once and for all. To her surprise and benefit, Monica was already having lunch with him, and her recording cell phone got an eye full. Seeing Mark with another woman hurt her to the core, but in her mind she thought he was lonely since they hadn't interacted in a few months. Undoubtedly he had been with Monica was before she had to "leave." Her mom had taken it upon herself, once again, to contact her doctor to find out how she'd being doing. Once she'd found out that "she" was off her meds again, the doctor insisted that she go back to that God awful "resort" to help make her better. When were they going to realize that she didn't need that resort or those meds? After all, she'd been doing just fine without them. Thanks to her mother and Shady Pine Mental Resort, she had missed the last four months of being with her man, and now he was finding comfort with *another* someone else.

***

Kayla headed to the office to meet with two patients before her doctor's appointment later that afternoon. She had forgotten to tell Mark about this one and accepted that she would have to go alone. Going into her office, she thought it would be a good idea to see if maybe he would come with her on his lunch break. Reflecting back on the perfume incident, she'd decided she would play her cards and see what proof she could get before confronting him again. Either way, if he told the truth and confirmed her suspicions, she knew her marriage would really be over this time. So instead of going off on a whim, she decided to get concrete proof before she tore her marriage apart.

Before she could get into the building good, Melissa called. She was calling to talk about the baby shower again. Kayla asked her several times to just call her mom since Vivian would know exactly what Kayla liked and didn't like, but Melissa insisted on calling her every other day. The shower was in two weeks, and Kayla couldn't wait for it to be over. The event was now up to one hundred guests and was at a banquet hall more suited for a wedding reception than a baby shower. Melissa even took the liberty of setting up registries at almost every store imaginable. The baby shower was way too much for Kayla's taste, but no matter what, she knew that Melissa always had an excuse as to why the event had to be so fabulous. Kayla just hoped that when she and Mark had more children, they didn't have to go through this every time.

With all of her morning patients seen and all notes finalized, Kayla headed out to get to Mark's office to see if he could go to the doctor with her. She already made up her mind that if he couldn't, it would be okay since she knew it was a last minute thing. It didn't take long for her to pull up to the office and head inside. It was twelve-forty, and her appointment was for one-thirty, so she had plenty of time to convince Mark to come and still get over to Dr. Gallant's office to be on time.

After getting off the elevator and heading to Mark's office, Kayla got a funny feeling in the pit of her stomach. She thought her mind was playing tricks on her, but it wasn't long before her nose confirmed that her mind was right. She locked her eyes on Monica and the scent of Light Blue perfume.

"Hey, Monica, how are you today?" Kayla asked with her nose turned up in the air.

Monica had a flash of discomfort before she presented a cool, calm, collected tone. "I'm doing well, Mrs. Barnes. Was Mr. Barnes expecting you? Because he just left for a 1:00 appointment," Monica stated calmly not missing a beat.

"He wasn't. I thought I'd surprise my *husband* today," Kayla said slowly, putting emphasis on the word husband as if Monica didn't know they were married.

"Oh, well I'm sure you can get him on his cell. He has the rest of the afternoon blocked off," Monica said. This time Kayla could sense a lingering discomfort in Monica.

"Of course I'll try his cell. I'm his wife. He'll always pick up," Kayla said cockily as she winked at Monica before she waddled away.

She walked to the elevator with so much anger in her steps that one would've thought she was a kid stomping to her room. Kayla knew that scent was familiar and couldn't believe it was right there. The affair that she'd cried herself to sleep over. The one that practically tore her marriage apart was not only right in her face all this time, but also right under her nose, and she had no idea. She never bothered to ask who it was. In her mind, who it was didn't matter. All that mattered was that it was someone else. She racked her brain on her way to Dr. Gallant's office, wondering why she never saw it before. She had been in that office in Monica's presence dozens of times and never once thought she was having an affair with her husband. Now it was all out in the open, and she couldn't wait to confront Mark about it.

***

"Is this what you wanted?! Huh?! Tell me you want it!"

Smack!

The smacking of the ass cheek caused it to jiggle just like Mark liked. This turned him on even more and caused him to go deeper.

Mark was pounding her from behind and enjoying every minute of it. He didn't know how he got here.

Actually, he did. He knew that meeting her at a hotel was a bad idea, but a part of him needed the release as bad as she wanted it. He still had no idea what picture she was planning to send his wife nor did he care at the moment. He was only concerned about the orgasm building inside of him. Not being able to control himself any longer, he released himself in the condom and slowly pulled out of her. Collapsing on the bed, he couldn't move if he wanted to. The two had been in the hotel room for hours, going at it. He missed all the wild freaky things she would do to and with him, but mostly he missed having sex without a belly in the way. He had to apologize to her for catching him with Monica to get the special attention he craved. He even went so far as to tell her that she was the best he'd ever had so she would lighten up. To his surprise, she forgave him and said she'd known that it was because she was gone for months. He made a mental note of the "gone for months" part but decided not to push it. Finally getting up the energy to release his bladder, he grabbed his cell phone on the way to the bathroom. He had thirty-seven missed calls and nineteen text messages. He opened the first one and saw it was from Monica.

Your wife came here. I think she knows. Call the office.

He shook his head, confused as to why she would think that. For the life of him, he couldn't imagine why she would think Kayla knew about them. He was always so careful, and they never talked outside of work. Quickly dismissing Monica's text, he opened the messages from Kayla. It was several of them, but the first one caught his attention and had him racing to get out of the hotel room.

"What the hell happened?!" she asked out loud as Mark sped by her.

One minute he was going to the bathroom, the next minute he was throwing his clothes on and running out the door. He didn't even give an explanation. He just said he would call her later. She lay on the bed and wondered what was going on. The ringing of her cell phone interrupted her thoughts. She thought about not answering, but then decided that maybe the caller could help with her recent thoughts.

Her suspicions were confirmed when Kayla screamed, "I'm in labor! Please come down here!"

Rolling her eyes at Kayla's dramatic yelling, she took her time getting up and showering before heading out of the hotel. She was in no rush to get to Kayla, but at least she knew where Mark rushed off to.

Chapter 11

Screaming was all you could hear as Mark stepped off the elevators at Mercy Hospital. The messages from Kayla caught him off guard completely. She was only seven and a half months, so the baby wasn't due yet. To the best of his knowledge, she wasn't being induced, and the pregnancy was normal, so he couldn't understand how or why she was in labor. The fact that she had been trying to reach him for hours was unnerving. He had no business being in that hotel room with Stephanie and to know that he was there with her while Kayla was having his son made him feel horrible. If anything happened to either one of them, he would never forgive himself.

Making his way to the nurse's station, he couldn't control his sweating or his hands from shaking. He was not only nervous about the delivery, but also about becoming a father and what would happen to his marriage. The walls were closing in on him, and he didn't know which way to go. After getting directions from the nurse and being escorted to a scrubbing area, he cleaned himself up, according to the directions he was given, and was escorted into the room just in time to see his son come into the world. Kayla was crowning when he walked in according to the nurse. There was so much commotion in the room that nobody seemed to notice his presence. Kayla was laid back on the bed with a nurse holding her hand while another one was wiping the sweat from her forehead and a slew of doctors and nurses standing by calling out numbers and directions. Mark's feet were glued to the floor and he had no idea what to do or say. In a matter of minutes, he began to see his son's body slide out of Kayla while she was screaming bloody murder. He wondered if she had gotten that epidural thing he'd heard women talk about. The way she was screaming was as if she was going cold turkey. The second Mark Anthony Barnes Jr. was out of her womb, the doctors started yelling things that he had no idea what it meant. All he noticed was that baby Mark was blue and something wasn't right. Parental instinct guided Mark, as his otherwise glued feet sprang into action and he was rushing to the doctors and nurses who were ushering his son out the room. Desperate for someone to say something, he grabbed the arm of the doctor who performed the delivery and asked what was wrong with his son.

"I'm sorry, sir, but he's crashing. We have to get him into emergency surgery."

And just like that the doctor rushed out the room leaving Mark behind.

***

Kayla didn't know what to do or say. There she was lying in a hospital bed after she'd just given birth to her son almost two months early. She went to see Dr. Gallant as scheduled, with thoughts of Mark's affair on her mind still. After examining her, Dr. Gallant informed her that her blood pressure was too high and the baby was in distress. She told Kayla that she had to induce her and deliver Mark Jr. today or he was in danger. Kayla immediately began calling Mark, but couldn't get a hold of him. She even called the office and told Monica what was going on and told her she needed to get a hold of Mark. Monica could not offer any information since there were no details on his calendar about where the meeting was or who it was with. Kayla thought that it was weird that Monica didn't have any information, but she didn't want to assume that she was so heartless that she would keep Mark away from her while she delivered their baby. Kayla also felt better knowing that Mark wasn't with Monica so she assumed Kayla's reasoning it was on the up and up.

***

Stephanie strolled into labor and delivery an hour later and gave the nurse Kayla's name. After being informed that she'd just delivered and wasn't taking visitors yet, Stephanie had a seat in the waiting area and began reading a magazine. She was in no mood to be mushy over a baby that was conceived by accident, but she would do her best at pretending for Mark's sake. This was the first time they'd hooked up in months and she didn't want to ruin the chance to pick back up where they'd left off. Besides, she didn't understand why Kayla called her anyway. They hadn't spoken since the day she came to pick up her things from her house. Thinking about that pissed Stephanie off even more. It's been months since they spoke to each other. Not a single text message or phone call. Yet, the second she has a crisis, she asks for Stephanie to be there for her once again.

She couldn't wait until Mark left her needy ass for good. She would be right there to rub it in little Miss Perfect's face that for once she got the man and the happy ending and then she would see what little Miss Psychology would do then.

***

Mark didn't know what to say to Kayla. She had just given birth to their son who was off having emergency surgery. Little did Kayla know, but he'd missed the beginning of her labor because he was in a hotel room banging her best friend.

Mark kissed Kayla on the top of her head. "You look beautiful. You did a great job."

Instead of smiling or squeezing his hand, she erupted in tears. Not knowing what to do, Mark stood up to go get some air. Before he was out the door, Kayla's voice stopped him in his tracks.

"I know you're sleeping with Monica," Kayla said slowly before she began crying again. "I want a divorce."

Mark couldn't get on the other side of the door quick enough. Not only was his adulterous ways catching up to him, but the truth about one of his flings' identity was out in the open.

"How in the hell did she know that?" he said, not realizing he was talking out loud.

"Know what?" Stephanie asked with a smirk on her face.

"Nothing, nothing!" Mark quickly said trying to avoid telling Stephanie the truth.

Of course, Stephanie had already known about Monica. After all, she walked in on the two of them at his office. He just didn't feel comfortable talking about what had just happened between he and his wife with Stephanie.

Monica wasn't the only other woman that Stephanie knew about it, though. The two of them had shared women before. It was

Stephanie's idea, but he was glad he'd gone along with it. Having two women please each other in front of him was every man's fantasy, and Mark had enjoyed it on more than one occasion.

Stephanie had a free sexual spirit. And although he enjoyed that about her while they were together, he knew it was also one of the reasons that he could never be with her exclusively. His dad had always told him that the woman that you make your wife should be as pure as possible. What Jack didn't tell him was that his wife would probably be as boring as possible too.

Mark knew he had to get away from Stephanie before he said something he would regret, so he made up a lie. "I have to go get Kayla something to eat."

Apparently lying had become his new favorite hobby, and he was getting better and better at it.

***

Stephanie eased into Kayla's room, still confused by what she'd overheard Mark saying in the hallway. She stood back to watch him, hoping that the mumbling he was doing meant they had something in common, and he had "people" telling him what to do as well. It would be perfect if he did. Then they could live happily ever after, and finally they would have no secrets between them. But once she got closer to him, she could tell something had just happened between him and Kayla, and that it was bothering him.

She walked over to a crying Kayla, and surprisingly she was genuinely concerned; not for Kayla, but for herself. She was hoping that the tears meant that Kayla was leaving Mark, and she was closer to getting him all to herself.

Sitting down next to Kayla, she was curious about the tears and faking her concern, "What's wrong, Kayla?"

Kayla stopped crying long enough to tell Stephanie about Mark's affair with Monica. "It was right in her face all along! I had no idea what was going on. I'm filing for a divorce as soon as possible." As she wiped her face, she turned and looked Stephanie in the eyes. "Steph, I just want to say that I am so sorry. I know we have been a little distant, and it's been months since the last time we spoke. I just want to say thank you for being a true friend to me. When Mark and I started having problems in our marriage, you were right there when I needed you. I can't thank you enough for letting me bend your ear and for holding my hand."

All kinds of things were going through Stephanie's head. She couldn't believe her ears. Kayla was divorcing Mark, and soon enough she would have him all to herself. She also made a note to take care of Monica. There was no way she could keep her around after the divorce. She knew her and Mark had history, but that was all they were going to have if Stephanie could help it. She didn't sit around in the wings this long waiting to have someone else come in and swoop Mark from up under her again. Stephanie had finally gotten her man after all these years, and nobody was going to get in her way of her happily ever after.

Chapter 12

Vivian helped Kayla get out of the car and into her house while William carried a sleeping MJ in his baby carrier. A week later and they were finally released from the hospital. Kayla felt fine, but Vivian insisted that she still had to be sore. William constantly expressed his disbelief that his baby girl had had a baby. Judging from the look in his eyes, as he admired MJ, one would think that MJ was his first and only grandchild. However, what he truly couldn't believe was that Mark had been cheating on his daughter. When she came to visit months ago, he knew something was wrong the moment he laid eyes on her. He never wanted to pry or insert himself in either one of his daughters' relationships unless they asked him to, so he made it a point to wait until she wanted to talk about things. When he got the news that she was pregnant, he had mixed emotions. He knew Kayla would make a terrific mother, but even then he was worried about the state of her marriage. When a few months went by, and he never heard anything else, he assumed that she and Mark had worked through their problems like he and Vivian had dozens of times before. Now here he was arriving at the hospital after she had had her first child, to find out that not only was their marriage not on the right track, but that they were getting a divorce. After William had seen Mark a few times at the hospital, he had to fight back the urge to confront him. He promised Kayla he wouldn't, but deep down he really didn't understand why Mark would sleep with his assistant behind Kayla's back. He also fought the urge to ask why Mark appeared to be so uncomfortable around Stephanie. From what

William knew, they were all supposed to be close and good friends, yet Mark made it a point to be nowhere near Stephanie while in the hospital and Stephanie made it a point to keep her eyes glued to Mark no matter where he went.

***

Getting in and comfortable, Kayla couldn't help but to be relieved that she was finally home. MJ's surgery was minor, and her baby proved to be a fighter. He was released to go with no special instructions or plans. His first appointment would be in a couple of days, but that was normal for a newborn. Kayla prayed every day while they were in the hospital that God wouldn't punish her son for her letting Mark's unfaithfulness get to her. Now, here she was at home with a baby that was healthy and happy and Kayla couldn't ask for more. She looked around and noticed that Mark had honored her request and began to move out before she came home. Divorce was never something Kayla expected to experience. Her marriage was supposed to be solid and last just as long as her parent's marriage had, but now here she was with a different scenario. She also noticed that she hadn't heard from Stephanie since she got out of the hospital. That was strange being that she was right by her side for the first few days until Kayla's parents arrived. Deciding she would call her later, Kayla decided to take a nap while her parents were still there. They would be leaving tomorrow, and once they were gone she had no idea when she would be able to sleep again.

DECEITFUL VOWS

***

Mark was a wreck. He didn't know what to do or where to go. He was laid up in his suite, at the Four Seasons, with Monica. Since Kayla had asked for a divorce, he didn't know how to occupy his time. Instead of trying to get back with his wife, he decided to, once again, fall victim to temptation's lust. Before a few days ago, he had never been intimate with Monica. He would just get blowjobs in his office. But now here he was laid up beside her in a hotel bed, having gone all the way with her. He knew that he would never get Kayla back this way, but he also knew that if he did. he would have to fire Monica. So he decided to enjoy her while he could.

***

Stephanie was fuming. She had followed Monica to Mark's hotel once again. It was the third day in a row. She knew that they were sleeping together because Monica walked around with that same glow that Stephanie would get after he made love to her. She knew she had to get rid of Monica, but she just didn't know how. She decided that if she confronted Monica she could get her to just quit and walk away, but the voices in her head were telling her that she needed to get rid of her for good. Stephanie knew if she listened to them she would have to go back to the resort, and she didn't want to do that and risk losing Mark for good.

She pulled off and headed home. She needed to take her meds and think of an idea to get Mark back and stay out of the resort.

***

After a night out with Monica, Mark stopped by Kayla's house to see MJ. Kayla made no attempt to hide her disappointment in him for the affair. She also made it a point to let him know beforehand what she would ask for in the divorce settlement. Mark felt horrible as he looked into his son's eyes. He knew that he would still be a great father, but he also knew his marriage was done. Raising his son in separate households wasn't ideal, but if it came to that he would do his best job at making sure MJ was healthy and happy and that Kayla had the least amount of worries.

Kayla was off pumping milk for his son's bottles. Although they were happily married just a few weeks ago, the truth was they were now separated, and she refused to pull her breast out and pump in front of him. The doorbell rang, and she called out for Mark to get it. Since she had been home, coworkers and Mark's family and friends had been stopping by to see MJ. Mark asked Kayla to let him break the divorce to his family, so whenever someone visited she would say he was working.

When Mark answered the door, he stood there stuck and frustrated.

"Well, are you going to let me in or what?" Stephanie asked highly annoyed with Mark's presence. She knew about him and Monica, yet he wasn't answering any of her calls or texts.

"Hello Stephanie," Mark responded with matching annoyance in his tone.

He didn't have any more interest in Stephanie, and he definitely wasn't in the mood for her nonsense with Kayla in the same space as them. He hoped for her sake she would be able to keep it together. If Stephanie let the truth slip out to Kayla, it would be hell to pay.

"Let her in Mark," Kayla said from behind them.

Kayla couldn't help but notice the startled look on both their faces when she spoke. It was almost like they had seen a ghost. She went to greet Stephanie with a hug and felt the obvious tension between them.

"You must have known that I was about to call your butt. I haven't heard from you since the hospital," Kayla said, playfully nudging Stephanie's arm.

"I was coming, damn. Chill out. You know I don't do hospitals." Stephanie said, with a slight smile.

"Well, that's cool, but you could've made an exception for your nephew."

"He is not her nephew," Mark spat.

Before Kayla could get a word out, Stephanie butted in and said, "He's right, Kayla. MJ is not my nephew, but he is my Godson, and I'm here now."

Those words should have put Kayla at ease, but she couldn't help but notice the tension in the room was thicker than usual. She remembered her mom telling her that her dad thought something was weird with Stephanie and Mark. Now Kayla was wondering if her dad was right. Noticing that MJ was asleep, she picked him up, took him upstairs and laid him down. Since she didn't intend on being out of work too long, she wanted to get him in the habit of sleeping in his crib so she wouldn't have a problem with him later. Once she laid him in the crib, she made certain to remove the stuffed animals from out of the crib and placed them on the dresser.

Starting towards the door to head back downstairs, Kayla was stalled with a conversation that suddenly filled that air that proved to be priceless.

"You don't know how to return calls or text now?" Kayla heard Stephanie attempt to whisper. Her voice was full of frustration.

"I do, just not yours. Can't you tell we are over?" Mark replied, matter-of-factly.

He had lowered his voice as well. He was as clueless as Stephanie that Kayla was eavesdropping on their conversation.

"We're over when I say we're over, so again I suggest you start answering the phone."

"Why can't you get it through your head that I don't want you?!" Mark's voice raised a bit. "I never wanted you!"

"You wanted me until Monica came along." Stephanie's voice was also starting to grow louder.

"You're nuts!" Mark said, in an angry whisper.

Kayla couldn't believe her ears. Stephanie was sitting in her living room, talking about sleeping with her husband while she was just upstairs putting MJ down for his nap.

"I'll show you nuts! I know you've been screwing her for the past couple of days. That's why you're not answering my calls. Kayla thinks it's just Monica, but wait until she hears about all the others."

"You wouldn't dare! Besides, how can you tell her about the others without telling about yourself?"

"She doesn't have to. I already know."

Stephanie and Mark both sat shocked and speechless. Neither of them had realized the baby monitor on the coffee table was present let alone turned on. Kayla had heard the entire conversation from the nursery. To say she was shocked was an understatement. She thought that they hated each other all long. Now finding out they had been having an affair, she didn't know which one she wanted to smack first.

"Stephanie, I can't believe you! You were supposed to be my best friend!" Kayla yelled.

She was now also crying hysterically from the betrayal of the two people in the world who were supposed to mean the most to her. Here she was just days after giving birth to a baby to find out her husband was cheating on her with her best friend! Had it not been for MJ, she would've tried to kill them both. Smelling his assistant on him that night was bad enough but at least she had no ties or connections to her so it wasn't personal, but Stephanie was her absolute best friend! She couldn't believe that she sat there time after time and listened to her go on and on about Mark all the while knowing that she was the other woman.

"After all we've been through, you slept with my husband behind my back! You let me cry on your shoulder and sleep in your home, all the while knowing it was your fault. Now it all makes sense why you've always thrown shade about Mark and why you weren't happy when I found out I was pregnant. You were jealous all along! You wanted him for yourself. But guess what? You can have him now. I don't want nothing to do with neither one of your lying asses!"

"Bravo, bravo, Miss Drama Queen, bravo!" Stephanie said while clapping her hands. "Are you done now? That was a great speech but then again you're always good at taking the spotlight. But let me ask you; how does it feel to know that little Miss Perfect isn't so perfect? It didn't take much convincing to get Mark in my bed. Hell, I told you he wasn't no good. I knew because I had him, and it wasn't just me. I hate to burst your bubble, but I've been sharing your husband all along."

Seeing the hurt in Kayla's face seemed to egg Stephanie on.

"Yep... we've had more threesomes than I can count, and he's been with other women on his own without me. so don't think for a second that things are just about you because they aren't."

Kayla had heard enough from Stephanie. So much so that she couldn't decipher what was real or fake. What she was certain of was that she didn't need to hear a word from Mark. She had heard enough and it was time for both of them to leave.

She walked over to the door and opened it. In the calmest voice, she could muster up she told them, "Get out."

Mark and Stephanie both looked confused at Kayla's sudden calmness. Mark left without looking her way, but Stephanie was sure to blow her a kiss before she made her exit. After closing the door, Kayla could hold back, no more, the inevitable flood of tears.

Chapter 13

Two months after finding out about her husband and her best friend's affair, Kayla decided it was time to move on. She filed for legal separation from Mark and had gone back to work within two weeks. She'd began to interview sitters for MJ and then decided it was best and easier if she could find a nanny instead who could come and stay with him during the day. This would keep MJ in his environment and possibly help to keep him from getting sick because he wouldn't be around any other germy children.

Another added bonus was that without having to drive him to a facility, Kayla could spend more time with him in the mornings. Looking for a nanny was a hard process. By the time the background checks came back, half of her choices were cut; more were cut during the phone screen, and nobody passed the face-to-face. Mark had expressed to her that he thought she was too overprotective, but she didn't care what he thought about anything these days. After the more recent interviews of five highly qualified nannies, he showed extreme frustration that she couldn't make a choice. He had the nerve to tell her that maybe it wasn't the nannies but that it was her. Kayla's response was full of ice at his apparent gall.

"Just because you would sleep with anyone doesn't mean I would allow just anyone to keep my son."

Mark appeared frustrated at Kayla's comment, but let it slide. He didn't say another word. After all, Kayla felt that he was the one that messed up.

***

Mark had finally gotten the hint that he wouldn't be getting back with Kayla, so he found an apartment not far from the house so that he could continue to visit with MJ as much as possible. He truly wanted to buy a new home, but there wasn't much available in the area, and he didn't want to move too far. Since the truth had come out, he decided to fire Monica, but not before he gave her a hefty final bonus and an even more generous severance package. He also hadn't heard from Stephanie, which was great. And if he could truly have his way, he surely would keep things just like that. He couldn't say that he was happy with his present life, but he had come to accept the consequences of his mistakes.

***

After staking out Mark's apartment for the third straight week, Stephanie was pleased to see that no new action had taken place. Since the separation, she was pleased to see that Mark didn't bring home any women. She knew that he needed time to cool off, and eventually he would get lonely, and she would be able to come comfort him, but for now she had to give him time. She still had to keep an eye on him to make sure he didn't find anyone to replace her, so following him around was now her daily routine. This worked out for her too because it gave her time to get rid of those God-awful meds. She didn't need them anymore, and she was glad that she could finally stop taking them so she could feel like her old self again.

***

Mark pulled up to his apartment complex with thoughts of having a drink and watching the basketball game. Work was becoming overwhelming as CEO and some days he regretted wanting to be the head guy in charge. He didn't regret the time he spent with MJ, but some days he wished that he was still under the same roof as him and Kayla so he wouldn't have to travel back and forth.

After grabbing his briefcase and the pizza he'd just picked up from Pizza Johns, he climbed out of his car and for a second he thought his eyes were playing tricks on him, but it wasn't long before he realized they weren't. He thought he'd seen her a few days ago, but wasn't sure. Now he was absolutely positive that, in fact, it was her.

"What is she up to?" Mark wondered as he headed upstairs to unwind.

***

"Dammit!" Stephanie screamed as she banged on her steering wheel uncontrollably. She'd never thought he would recognize her. She'd traded in her Mercedes for a Honda Accord after she took a leave of absence from her agency. She had taken a one year unpaid personal leave the last time her mom had sent her to the resort. She thought a year would be long enough to win Mark's heart, get pregnant and get

87

back to work. She could surely afford to live off her savings that long, but the plan was that she wouldn't have to. She was supposed to be living happily ever after with Mark. Not worrying about anything except having babies. But instead she was staking out his apartment, hoping that he didn't have another one of his conquests coming over.

***

Being a single mother was getting hard for Kayla, even though money wasn't the issue. She had the finances to cover whatever MJ wanted or needed. The late night feedings, early morning diaper changes, and the crying fits were exhausting. She had no relief or reprieve from any of it. Mark came over three times a week to visit, but of course he got the bath time smiles, giggles and a feeding. If he was lucky, a diaper change. To him, MJ was a ball of fun and parenting was easy breezy, but if only he knew what it was really like.

Kayla and Mark finally agreed on a nanny. Her name was Virginia, and she was a forty-eight-year-old caregiver. Virginia had given birth to three kids of her own by the age of twenty. Once they were grown and on their own, she finally knew what she would do with the rest of life.

She started out watching her girlfriend's kids as a way to make extra money when her kids were younger. Because she didn't work, she had a lot of extra time on her hands. The money that the state provided every month wasn't enough to take care of everything, so babysitting helped make the ends meet. It wasn't long before she realized she enjoyed caring for children and wanted to do it full time. Once her children were grown, Virginia was free to search for other children to help raise. She worked in a few daycare centers but felt they weren't nurturing enough. It wasn't long before she left and went to work for the Fosters, caring for their only child, a son named Martin. She took care of Martin until he was sixteen years old. After that, they didn't really need Virginia anymore, so she set out to find another family to help. Virginia was still close to the Fosters, and they even sent her a small check once a month to help her out until she found work again.

***

Kayla was up early getting ready for work. It had been almost four months since her leave started, and she was anxious and nervous as if it was her first day on the job. She didn't know what to expect from her patients and coworkers alike. Before she left, she was happily married and expecting her first child. Now she was returning; separated and a single parent. Talk about the tables turning. With the separation from Mark, Kayla didn't have any other duties besides caring for MJ, so she was able to get in her home gym and get her "snapback" in order. It was virtually unbelievable that she had an almost three-month-old son at home, looking at her body. She decided to wear a black form-fitting suit with a red lace blouse and her favorite patent leather Louboutins. Even though her body was back to pre-baby shape, she decided to wear black to give her frame an even more slimming look. Since MJ had her up late the night before, she decided to cover the bags under her eyes with a little foundation and eyeliner. Her hair had grown a lot during her pregnancy, so she wore it in an updo. It was her only option being that she'd meant to make a trip to Sue, her stylist, and get a cute cut. But for now the high bun would have to do the trick.

Heading downstairs to find Virginia already feeding MJ, Kayla decided that it was best to just grab her lunch bag and go. She would have to stop and get coffee on her way in because if she stayed home any longer she wouldn't have been able to actually leave MJ.

Surprisingly Kayla did well for her first day back. Her patients actually found her more relatable and down to earth since she was no longer wearing a wedding band. She had only used FaceTime twice to check on how well MJ was doing with Virginia. Even when Mark called to see how she was holding up, she took the call like a champ. Although she missed her baby terribly, she had to admit she wasn't a nervous wreck like she'd thought she would be. The morning and early afternoon went smoothly until around two-thirty when things got ugly.

"Kayla, get home now! It's urgent! I'm on my way there!"

She couldn't get a word in edgewise before Mark hung up.

Click.

Kayla didn't know what to do or say. Her instincts kicked in, and she immediately grabbed her purse and flew out of the office. She paused for a brief moment to tell her assistant that she was gone for the day and would not be back. She pretended to ignore the sound of the young girl smacking her lips at her statement. Kayla didn't even know where she came from or who hired her and didn't much care at the time. Rebecca was her assistant before she went on maternity leave. Sometimes they switched personnel to make easier accommodations, so Kayla didn't think anything of it. But after working with Latoya for just half a day, she knew this arrangement wouldn't last long at all.

Kayla sped all the way home, doing at least eighty-five miles per hour on the highway. She made the usual forty-five minute drive in twenty minutes. She attempted to call Mark back several times but didn't get an answer. Once she pulled up to her home and saw cop cars everywhere, her heart started racing and everything instantly became blurred through the tears. Once she saw the ambulance come out with a gurney, she lost all focus of her car, and everything went black.

Chapter 14

Coming to, Kayla realized she was in a hospital bed. She instantly began to panic and scan the room. The monitors connected to her were going crazy and beeping uncontrollably until she laid her eyes on Mark and MJ. The sight of them calmed her down and made the machines come back to a somewhat normal pace.

"Your mom is on her way. I called her a while ago," Mark said, barely above a whisper since he was holding a sleeping MJ. "I waited until I got word from the doctor so that I could assure her that you were okay, and she wouldn't rush here in fear." He stood and walked MJ close to Kayla so she could see his sleeping face. She was on so much muscle relaxer and pain medicine the doctors advised that she not hold the baby out of fear that she may drop him.

"What happened? Why am I here?" Kayla asked.

"Yeah, Mark, tell us what happened," Vivian said through gritted teeth from the doorway to the hospital room.

Vivian was pissed that once again she was back at the hospital with her daughter due to some damage that Mark had caused. Yes, the first time she got her grandson out of it, but this time she couldn't imagine why her daughter was here. All she knew was Mark was the reason behind it and this time she wasn't leaving until she got this situation under control once and for all. Vivian stood in the doorway with her hand on her hip, waiting for a response. Had Mark not been holding MJ, she would've slapped the taste out of his mouth, she was just that angry. Luckily for him, MJ saved him, but if his response wasn't up to par, MJ wouldn't be able to save him again.

Realizing that both Vivian and Kayla were waiting for a response, Mark stood up and placed a sleeping MJ in his car seat before he began the story of how Kayla got in that hospital bed.

"I was in my office working when Steve told me that I had a call."

Mark wanted to elaborate on the fact that Steve was his new assistant so that Kayla could take notice that he had intentionally hired a male. That was in case she ever wanted to take him back. But considering the situation at hand, he figured he should continue on with the story.

"I took the call and soon found out it was Stephanie's mother. She was worried about her because she hadn't heard from her in a few months. She said that usually when that happened, she was off her meds, so she worried about her. At first she said she ignored it since Stephanie was just released a couple months prior and just assumed that she was getting things back in order."

Mark could see the confused look on both Kayla and Vivian's face. Obviously, no one had known of Stephanie's illness. But he appreciated that they didn't interrupt him. So he continued to talk.

"She said that once Stephanie's doctor called and told her that she hadn't filled any of her prescriptions, she knew something was wrong, so she tried to call her, but Stephanie wouldn't answer."

"That doesn't explain why *I'm* here!" Kayla screamed. Her tone was full of annoyance and frustration.

Mark took another deep breath and continued. "After a few days of not getting an answer when she called, her mother decided to locate her cell phone. Apparently, when she had Stephanie committed the last time, she installed a locator app on her cell so she would always be able to pinpoint her location if she ever went off her meds again. Good that she did because she was able to see that she had been camped out between my place and your place for months now. I saw her at my place a couple times, but I didn't think anything of it. I had no idea she was watching you and MJ."

"Oh my God," Kayla cried. "Knowing that someone has been following and watching me and I had no idea? I never knew that Stephanie was crazy. Oh, thank God MJ was not hurt. But what now? Will Stephanie try this again, Mark?" Kayla asked for reassurance.

"Well, her mom called me because she had me listed as her emergency contact while she was in Shady Pines. Once she told me the address, I told her that one was mine, and the other was the house you live in with MJ. Her mom instantly began to panic and told me to hurry there and call 911 on my way. So after I called the cops, I called you and told you to come home. Her mom called back and told me that Stephanie had told her that she was getting married and would need a babysitter while we went on a honeymoon. When I mentioned MJ, she immediately assumed that that was the child she wanted her to watch. She was afraid she would harm you, so that's why she told me to call the police."

"But that doesn't make sense. Kayla wasn't even home and if she was staking the place out she knew that," Vivian said in disbelief.

"Her plan was to kidnap MJ. She was going to blackmail me into running off and marrying her. If I would've refused, she was going to threaten to hurt him. She wanted Kayla to lose both MJ and me. She knew Virginia was there but didn't assume she would put up a fight when she tried to take MJ. She assumed that since she was just a nanny and it was her first day, it would be easy to get MJ, but Virginia tried to block the stairs. That's when she stabbed Virginia with a letter opener."

"That's who I saw on the stretcher?! That was the last thing I

94

remember. Then everything went dark, and I woke up here," Kayla exclaimed in recollection.

"Yes, you saw Virginia. After Stephanie stabbed her, she went and grabbed MJ but when she tried to leave, the cops were at the door. She threatened to stab herself if they didn't let her go, but they apprehended her first and got MJ. I guess that's when you hit the tree and blacked out. Your car went up on the curb, and the steering wheel knocked you unconscious when you hit it. Virginia is going to be okay. The wounds weren't life threatening. Stephanie's mom said that she's coming to make sure they put her in a proper mental facility and not release her this time. She said she's been suffering from schizophrenia since she was a child. She seemed to have it under control once, but after her dad died she went off the deep end. Her mother thinks that's where her obsession with men came from."

Both Kayla and her mother seemed stomped after hearing that story. None of Mark's behaviors were justified, but now Kayla felt a twinge of remorse because she was the one that had Stephanie involved in their lives from the beginning. She also knew that had it not been for Stephanie, she would've never met Mark. In a matter of months, her whole life was turned upside down, and she couldn't figure out how to put things back in place. Kayla went off into deep thought while Mark watched her intently.

As if she knew they needed to talk, Vivian excused herself to go get coffee. Once Vivian was gone, Mark took the opportunity to speak.

"Kayla, being that close to losing you and my son only made me realize that our home should be all that I need. These last few months, I promise I haven't seen Monica or Stephanie, or anyone else for that matter; I have been so content. I just want to be on the up and up with you, and maybe things won't be so bad. I love you, Kayla.

Kayla listened intently. Tears were threatening to fall from her eyes at the words that escaped from Mark's lips.

"Kayla, baby, I know I haven't been the best husband to you. I've done some things I'm not proud of, and I've hurt you. I never loved another woman the way I love you, and I could never imagine spending my life with anyone other than you and my son. I know it seems hard now, but if you give me one more chance, I promise to do right by you and MJ and never bring another tear to your eyes, unless it's a tear of joy. I promise to be the husband to you that I vowed to be on our wedding day. I promise to love, honor, obey and be nothing but faithful to you. Kayla Barnes, please forgive me and give our family another chance."

By now, both Mark and Kayla had tears coming down their faces. Those words and that reassurance was what Kayla had needed to hear months ago. Hearing him finally admit his wrongs and faults and asking for his family back sounded like music to Kayla's ears. Unfortunately, her heart didn't like the song so when she opened her mouth to respond to his confession of love for her, neither of them were prepared for what she said.

"Mark, my love for you is unconditional. You've shown me things I've never seen before and gave me my first born child. That alone puts a special place in my heart for you that I can never forget. Being married to you has shown and taught me a lot of things, but the most important thing I've learned from my time with you is that your vows to me on our wedding day were nothing but a joke. Now, these promises you're making to me today sound like an even bigger joke. Since the day we met, you've seemed to do nothing but give me worthless promises and vows, and I've had enough." Kayla finalized her speech with, "I want a divorce!"

THE END!

CONTACT INFORMATION

Facebook: Author A Mackin

Instagram: author_alice

Email: amackinwriter@yahoo.com

CPSIA information can be obtained at www.ICGtesting.com
Printed in the USA
LVOW07s2349310715

448467LV00019B/984/P